POLLYANNA

by Eleanor H. Porter

abridged for young readers

Abridged from *Pollyanna* by Eleanor H. Porter, first published in 1913.

Editor: John Holdren

Art Director: Steve Godwin

Designer: Jayoung Cho

Illustrator: Jayoung Cho

ISBN: 1-931728-41-0

POLLYANNA

POLLYANNA

by Eleanor H. Porter

1. MISS POLLY

Miss Polly Harrington entered her kitchen a little hurriedly this June morning. Miss Polly did not usually make hurried movements. She prided herself on her repose of manner. But today she was hurrying—actually hurrying.

Nancy, washing dishes at the sink, looked up in surprise. Nancy had been working in Miss Polly's kitchen only two months, but already she knew that her mistress did not usually hurry.

"Nancy!"

"Yes, ma'am," Nancy answered cheerfully, but continued wiping the pitcher in her hand.

"Nancy,"—Miss Polly's voice was very stern now—"when I'm talking to you, I wish you to stop your work and listen to what I have to say."

Nancy set the pitcher down at once, nearly tipping it over. "Yes, ma'am, I will, ma'am," she stammered. "I was only keepin' on with my work 'cause you specially told me this mornin' to hurry with my dishes."

Miss Polly frowned. "That will do, Nancy. I did not ask for explanations. I asked for your attention."

"Yes, ma'am." Nancy wondered if she could ever please this woman. She had been so pleased when she found a place in the kitchen of the great house on the hill—Nancy had come from "The Corners," six miles away, and she knew Miss Polly Harrington only as one of the wealthiest residents of the town. That was two months before. She knew Miss Polly now as a stern, severe-faced woman who frowned if a knife clattered to the floor, or if a door banged—but who never thought to smile even when knives and doors were still.

"When you've finished your morning work, Nancy," Miss Polly was saying now, "you may clear the little room at the head of the stairs in the attic, and make up the cot bed. I may as well tell you now, Nancy. My niece, Miss Pollyanna Whittier, is coming to live with me. She is eleven years old, and will sleep in that room."

"A little girl—coming here, Miss Harrington? Oh, won't that be nice!" cried Nancy.

"Nice? Well, that isn't exactly the word I should use," said Miss Polly, stiffly. "However, I am a good woman, I hope, and I know my duty."

"Of course, ma'am. It was only that I thought a little girl here might—might brighten things up for you."

"Thank you," replied the lady, dryly. "I can't say, however, that I see any need for that."

"But, of course, you—you'd want her, your sister's child," said Nancy.

Miss Polly lifted her chin haughtily. "Well, really, Nancy, just because I happened to have a sister who was silly enough to marry and bring unnecessary children into the world, I can't see how I should want to care for them myself. However, as I said before, I hope I know my duty," she finished sharply, as she left the room.

"Yes, ma'am," sighed Nancy.

In her own room, Miss Polly took out the letter she had received two days before from the faraway Western town, and which had been so unpleasant a surprise to her. The letter was addressed to Miss Polly Harrington, Beldingsville, Vermont, and it read as follows:

Dear Madam:

I regret to inform you that the Reverend John Whittier died two weeks ago, leaving one child, a girl eleven years old. He left practically nothing else except a few books. As you know, he was the pastor of this small mission church, and had a very meager salary.

I believe he was your deceased sister's husband, but I understand the families were not on the best of terms. He thought, however, that for your sister's sake you might wish to take the child and bring her up among her own people in the East.

If you can take her, we would appreciate it very much. There is a man and his wife here who are going East very soon, and they would take her with them to Boston, and put her on the Beldingsville train.

Hoping to hear favorably from you soon, I remain,

Respectfully yours,
Jeremiah O. White

With a frown Miss Polly folded the letter and tucked it into its envelope. She had answered it and said she would take the child, of course. She hoped she knew her duty— disagreeable as the task would be.

As she sat now, her thoughts went back to her sister, Jennie, who had been this child's mother. Jennie, as a girl of twenty, had insisted upon marrying the young minister, in spite of her family's objections. There had been a man with more years, as well as more money, who had wanted to marry her. The minister had only a young head full of ideals and a heart full of love. Jennie had preferred these, so she had married the minister.

Miss Polly remembered it well, though she had been but a girl of fifteen at the time. Jennie had written, for a while, and had named her last baby "Pollyanna" for her two sisters, Polly and Anna. The other babies had all died. This had been the last time that Jennie had written. In a few years there had come the news of her death, told in a short, heartbroken little note from the minister.

Meanwhile, time had not stood still. Miss Polly was forty now, and quite alone in the world. Father, mother, sisters—all were dead. People had urged her to have some friend or companion live with her. She was not lonely, she said. She liked being by herself. She preferred quiet. But now—

Miss Polly rose with a frowning face. She was glad that she not only knew her duty, but also had strength to perform it. But—POLLYANNA!—what a ridiculous name!

2. Old Tom and Nancy

In the little attic room Nancy swept and scrubbed vigorously, paying special attention to the corners. "I—just—wish—I could—dig—out the corners—of—her—soul!" she muttered. "The idea of stickin' that blessed child 'way off up here in this hot little room—with no fire in the winter, too, and all this big house to pick and choose from! Unnecessary children, indeed! Humph!"

In the garden that afternoon, Nancy found Old Tom, who had pulled the weeds and shoveled the paths about the place for many years.

"Mr. Tom," began Nancy. "Did you know a little girl was comin' here to live with Miss Polly?"

"Go on with your jokin'," said the old man. "Why don't you tell me the sun is goin' to set in the east tomorrow?"

"But it's true. She told me so herself. It's her niece, and she's eleven years old."

The man's jaw fell. Then a tender light came into his faded eyes. "Why, Nancy, it must be Miss Jennie's little gal. Glory be!"

"Who was Miss Jennie?"

"She was an angel straight out of Heaven. She was twenty when she married and went away from here long years ago. Her babies all died, I heard, except the last one. And that must be the one that's a-comin'."

"And she's goin' to sleep in the attic!" scolded Nancy.

Old Tom frowned. The next moment a curious smile curved his lips. "I wonder what Miss Polly will do with a child in the house," he said.

"Well, I wonder what a child will do with Miss Polly in the house!" snapped Nancy.

The old man laughed. "I'm afraid you ain't fond of Miss Polly," he grinned.

"As if anybody could ever be fond of her!" scorned Nancy.

Old Tom stooped and began to work again. "I guess maybe you didn't know about Miss Polly's love affair," he said slowly.

"Love affair—HER! No!"

"Oh, yes," nodded the old man. "And the feller's livin' today, right in this town, too."

"Who is he?"

"I ain't a-tellin' that. It ain't fit that I should."

"But it don't seem possible," insisted Nancy.

Old Tom shook his head. "You didn't know Miss Polly as I did," he argued. "She used to be real handsome. She would be now, if she'd let herself be."

"Handsome! Miss Polly!"

"Yes. If she'd just let that tight hair of hers all loose, as it used to be, and wear lace and white things—you'd see she'd be handsome! Miss Polly ain't old, Nancy."

"Ain't she, though? Well, then she's got an awfully good imitation of it!" sniffed Nancy.

"Yes, I know. It begun then—at the time of the trouble with that feller," nodded Old Tom. "Ever since, she's been bitter an' prickly."

"I should say she was," declared Nancy. "There's no pleasin' her, no matter how you try!"

"Nancy!" called a sharp voice.

"Y-yes, ma'am," stammered Nancy, and hurried toward the house.

3. THE COMING OF POLLYANNA

A telegram announced that Pollyanna would arrive in Beldingsville the next day at four o'clock. Miss Polly read the telegram, frowned, then climbed the stairs to the attic room.

The room contained a small bed, two straight-backed chairs, a washstand, a bureau without any mirror, and a small table. There were no curtains and no pictures on the wall. All day the sun had been pouring down upon the roof, and the little room was like an oven. There were no screens, so the windows had not been raised. A big fly was buzzing angrily at one of them now, up and down, trying to get out.

Miss Polly killed the fly, straightened a chair, frowned again, and left the room.

"Nancy," she said a few minutes later, "I found a fly in Miss Pollyanna's room. The window must have been raised at some time. I have ordered screens, but until they come, the windows are to remain closed. My niece will arrive tomorrow at four o'clock. I want you to meet her at the station. Timothy will take the open buggy and drive you over. The telegram says 'light hair, red-checked gingham dress, and straw hat.'"

"Yes, ma'am, but—but—aren't you—"

Miss Polly frowned and said crisply, "No, I shall not go. It is not necessary that I should, I think. That is all." And she turned away.

The next afternoon, Timothy and Nancy drove off in the open buggy. Timothy was Old Tom's son. He was a good-natured youth, and a good-looking one as well.

Over and over in her mind, Nancy was saying, "Light hair, red-checked dress, straw hat." Over and over again she was wondering just what sort of child this Pollyanna might be.

"I hope for her sake she's quiet and sensible, and don't drop knives nor bang doors," she sighed to Timothy.

"Well, if she ain't, nobody knows what'll become of the rest of us," grinned Timothy. "Imagine Miss Polly and a NOISY kid!"

It was not long before they saw her—the slender little girl in the red-checked gingham with two braids of flaxen hair

hanging down her back. Beneath the straw hat, an eager, freckled little face turned to the right and to the left, plainly searching for someone.

Nancy knew the child at once. "Are you Miss—Pollyanna?" she asked. The next moment she found herself half smothered in the clasp of two gingham-clad arms.

"Oh, I'm so glad, *glad*, GLAD to see you," cried an eager voice in her ear. "Of course I'm Pollyanna, and I'm so glad you came to meet me! I hoped you would."

"You—you did?" stammered Nancy.

"Oh, yes, and I've been wondering all the way here what you looked like," cried the little girl, dancing on her toes. "And now I know, and I'm glad you look just like you do look."

Nancy was relieved to have Timothy come up. Pollyanna's words had been most confusing. "This is Timothy. Maybe you have a trunk," she stammered.

"Yes, I have," nodded Pollyanna. "I've got a brand-new one. The Ladies' Aid bought it for me. And wasn't it lovely of them, when they wanted the carpet so? Of course I don't know how much red carpet a trunk could buy, but it ought to buy some, anyhow. Much as half an aisle, don't you think? I've got a little thing here in my bag that Mr. Gray said was a check, and that I must give it to you before I could get my trunk. Mr. Gray is Mrs. Gray's husband. They're cousins of Deacon Carr's wife. I came East with them, and they're lovely! And—there, here 'tis," she finished, producing the check after much fumbling in her bag.

Nancy drew a long breath. She felt that someone had to breathe after that speech.

They were off at last, with Pollyanna snug between Nancy and Timothy. The little girl kept up an uninterrupted stream of comments and questions.

"There! Isn't this lovely? Is it far? I hope 'tis—I love to ride," sighed Pollyanna. "Of course, if it isn't far, I shan't mind, though, 'cause I'll be glad to get there all the sooner, you know. What a pretty street! I knew 'twas going to be pretty. Father told me—"

She stopped with a little choking breath. Nancy saw that her small chin was quivering, and that her eyes were full of tears. In a moment, however, she hurried on, bravely lifting her head.

"Father told me all about it. He remembered. And—and I ought to have explained before, about this red gingham dress, and why I'm not in black. There weren't any black things in the last missionary barrel. Part of the Ladies' Aid wanted to buy me a black dress and hat, but the other part thought the money ought to go toward the carpet they're trying to get—for the church, you know."

Pollyanna paused for breath. Nancy stammered, "Well, I'm sure it—it'll be all right."

"I'm glad you feel that way. I do, too," nodded Pollyanna. "Of course, it would have been a good deal harder to be glad in black—"

"Glad!" gasped Nancy.

"Yes—glad that father's gone to Heaven to be with mother and the rest of us, you know. He said I must be glad. But it's been pretty hard to do it, even in red gingham, because I—I wanted him so. And I couldn't help feeling I *ought* to have him, specially as mother and the rest have God and all the angels, while I didn't have anybody but the Ladies' Aid. But now I'm sure it'll be easier because I've got you, Aunt Polly. I'm so glad I've got you!"

"Oh, but—but you've made an awful mistake, dear," Nancy cried. "I'm only Nancy. I ain't your Aunt Polly at all!"

"You—you aren't?" stammered the little girl, in plain dismay.

"No. I'm only Nancy. I never thought of your takin' me for her. We—we ain't a bit alike!"

Timothy chuckled softly.

"But who ARE you?" questioned Pollyanna. "You don't look a bit like a Ladies' Aider!"

Timothy laughed outright this time.

"I'm Nancy, the hired girl. I do all the work except the washin' an' hard ironin'."

"But there IS an Aunt Polly?" asked the child, anxiously.

"You bet your life there is," cut in Timothy.

Pollyanna sighed. "Oh, that's all right, then." Then she went on brightly, "I'm glad, after all, that she didn't come to meet me, because now I've got her still coming, and I've got you besides. You know she's all the aunt I've got. And I didn't know I had her for ever so long. Then father told me. He said she lived in a lovely great big house on top of a hill."

"She does. You can see it now," said Nancy. "It's that big white one way ahead."

"Oh, how pretty! And what a lot of trees and grass all around it! I never saw such a lot of green grass all at once. Is my Aunt Polly rich, Nancy?"

"Yes, Miss."

"I'm so glad. It must be perfectly lovely to have lots of money. I never knew anyone that did have, only the Whites. They have carpets in every room and ice cream Sundays. Does Aunt Polly have ice cream Sundays?"

Nancy shook her head. "No, Miss. Your aunt don't like ice cream, I guess."

Pollyanna's face fell. "Oh, doesn't she? I'm so sorry! I don't see how she can help liking ice cream. But—anyhow, I can be glad about that, 'cause the ice cream you don't eat can't make your stomach ache like Mrs. White's did. Maybe Aunt Polly has got the carpets, though."

"Yes, she's got the carpets."

"In every room?"

"Well, in almost every room," answered Nancy, frowning at the thought of that bare little attic room with no carpet.

"Oh, I'm so glad," cried Pollyanna. "I love carpets. We didn't have any, only two little rugs that came in a missionary barrel, and one of those had ink spots on it. Mrs. White had pictures, too, perfectly beautiful ones of roses and little girls kneeling and a kitty and some lambs and a lion— not together, you know—the lambs and the lion. Don't you just love pictures?"

"I—I don't know," answered Nancy.

"I do. We didn't have any pictures. They don't come in the barrels much, you know. Two did come once, but one was so good father sold it to get money to buy me some shoes with. And the other was so bad it fell to pieces just as soon as we hung it up. And I cried. But I'm glad now we didn't have any of those nice things, 'cause I shall like Aunt Polly's all the better. My! Isn't this a perfectly beautiful house?" she broke off as they turned into the wide driveway.

As Timothy was unloading the trunk, Nancy muttered low in his ear, "I guess that blessed child will be needin' some rock to fly to for refuge. Well, I'm goin' to be that rock, Timothy. I am, I am!" she vowed, as she turned and led Pollyanna up the broad steps.

4. THE LITTLE ATTIC ROOM

Miss Polly Harrington did not rise to meet her niece. She looked up from her book as Nancy and the little girl appeared in the doorway. She held out a hand with "duty" written large on every coldly extended finger.

"How do you do, Pollyanna? I—" She had no chance to say more. Pollyanna flew across the room and flung herself into her aunt's lap.

"Oh, Aunt Polly, Aunt Polly, I don't know how to be glad enough that you let me come to live with you," she was sobbing. "You don't know how perfectly lovely it is to have you and Nancy and all this after you've had just the Ladies' Aid!"

"Very likely," said Miss Polly stiffly, trying to unclasp the small, clinging fingers, and turning frowning eyes on Nancy in the doorway. "Nancy, that will do. You may go. Pollyanna, be good enough, please, to stand in a proper manner. I don't know yet what you look like."

Pollyanna drew back at once. "I'm not very much to look at, anyway," she said, "on account of the freckles. Oh, and I ought to explain about the red gingham dress. I told Nancy how father said—"

"Yes. Well, never mind now what your father said," interrupted Miss Polly. "You had a trunk, I presume?"

"Oh, yes, indeed, Aunt Polly. I've got a beautiful trunk that the Ladies' Aid gave me. I haven't got so very much in it—of my own, I mean. The barrels haven't had many clothes for little girls in them lately. But there were all father's books, and Mrs. White said she thought I ought to have those. You see, father—"

"Pollyanna," her aunt broke in sharply, "there is one thing that might just as well be understood at once. I do not care to have you keep talking of your father to me. Now, we will go upstairs to your room. Your trunk is already there, I presume. I told Timothy to take it up."

Without speaking, Pollyanna turned and followed her aunt from the room. Her eyes were brimming with tears, but her chin was bravely high.

"After all, I—I reckon I'm glad she doesn't want me to talk about father," Pollyanna was thinking. "It'll be easier, maybe—if I don't talk about him. Probably, anyhow, that is why she told me not to talk about him."

Pollyanna blinked off the tears and looked eagerly about her. She was on the stairway now. Behind her an open door allowed a glimpse of soft-tinted rugs and satin-covered chairs. Beneath her feet the marvelous carpet felt like green moss. On every side the gilt of picture frames or the glint of sunlight through the lace curtains flashed in her eyes.

"Oh, Aunt Polly, Aunt Polly," breathed the little girl, "what a perfectly lovely, lovely house! How awfully glad you must be you're so rich!"

"Pollyanna!" exclaimed her aunt, turning sharply about as she reached the head of the stairs. "I'm surprised at you— making a speech like that to me!"

"Why, Aunt Polly, *aren't* you rich?" asked Pollyanna.

"Pollyanna, I hope I shall never be sinfully proud of any gift the Lord has seen fit to bestow upon me," declared the lady.

Miss Polly turned and walked down the hall toward the attic stairway door. She was glad that she had decided to put the child in the attic room. She wanted to get her niece as far as possible from herself, and place her where her childish carelessness would not destroy valuable furnishings.

Pollyanna's small feet pattered eagerly behind her aunt. Still more eagerly her big blue eyes tried to look in all directions at once in order not to miss anything. Most eagerly of all, her mind wondered behind which of all these fascinating doors her room was waiting—the beautiful room full of curtains, rugs, and pictures, that was to be her very own. Then, abruptly, her aunt opened a door and climbed another stairway.

A bare wall rose on either side. Trunks and boxes were stacked where the roof met the floor. It was hot and stifling. Then she saw her aunt open a door at the right.

"Pollyanna, here is your room, and your trunk is here, I see. Have you your key?"

Pollyanna nodded. Her eyes were wide and frightened.

Her aunt frowned. "When I ask a question, Pollyanna, I prefer that you should answer aloud, not merely with your head."

"Yes, Aunt Polly."

"Thank you. That is better. I believe you have everything that you need here," she added. "I will send Nancy up to help you unpack. Supper is at six o'clock."

For a moment after she had gone Pollyanna stood quite still. Then she turned her wide eyes to the bare wall, the bare floor, the bare windows. She turned them last to the little trunk that had stood not so long before in her own little room in the faraway Western home. Then she fell on her knees at its side, covering her face with her hands.

Nancy found her there when she came up a few minutes later. "There, there, you poor lamb," she crooned, drawing the little girl into her arms. "I was afraid I'd find you like this."

Pollyanna shook her head. "I'm bad and wicked, Nancy—awful wicked," she sobbed. "I just can't make myself understand that God and the angels needed my father more than I did."

"There, there, child," said Nancy. "Come, let's have your key. We'll get inside this trunk and take out your dresses in no time."

Tearfully, Pollyanna gave her the key. "There aren't very many there, anyway," she said.

"Then they're all the sooner unpacked," declared Nancy.

Pollyanna gave a sudden smile. "That's so! I can be glad of that, can't I?" she cried.

Nancy stared. "Why, of—course," she answered uncertainly.

Nancy quickly unpacked the books, the patched undergarments, and the few pitiful dresses. Pollyanna, smiling bravely now, flew about, hanging the dresses in the closet, stacking the books on the table, and putting the undergarments in the drawers.

"I'm sure it—it's going to be a very nice room. Don't you think so?" she stammered.

There was no answer. Nancy seemed very busy, with her head in the trunk. Pollyanna gazed at the bare wall above. "And I can be glad there isn't any looking-glass here, too, 'cause where there isn't any glass, I can't see my freckles."

Nancy made an odd little sound with her mouth, but when Pollyanna turned, her head was in the trunk again. At one of the windows, a few minutes later, Pollyanna gave a glad cry.

"Oh, Nancy, I hadn't seen this before," she breathed. "Look—way off there, with those trees and the houses and that lovely church spire, and the river shining just like silver. Why, Nancy, who needs pictures with that to look at? Oh, I'm so glad now she let me have this room!"

To Pollyanna's surprise, Nancy burst into tears. Pollyanna hurriedly crossed to her side.

"Why, Nancy, Nancy—what is it?" she cried. "This wasn't your room, was it?"

"My room!" stormed Nancy, choking back the tears. "If you ain't a little angel straight from Heaven. Oh, land! There's her bell!" Nancy sprang to her feet and went clattering down the stairs.

Pollyanna went back to her "picture," as she called the beautiful view from the window. She could not stand the stifling heat any longer. To her joy, the window frame moved under her fingers. The next moment it was wide open, and Pollyanna leaned far out, drinking in the fresh, sweet air.

She ran then to the other window. That, too, soon flew up under her eager hands. A big fly swept past her nose and buzzed noisily about the room. Then another came, and another. But Pollyanna paid no heed. She had made a wonderful discovery. Just outside this window, a huge tree flung its great branches. To Pollyanna they looked like arms stretched out and inviting her.

Suddenly she laughed aloud. "I believe I can do it," she chuckled. Then she climbed to the window ledge. From there it was easy to step to the nearest branch. Then, clinging like a monkey, she swung herself from limb to limb until she reached the lowest branch. The drop to the ground was a little scary, even for Pollyanna, who was used to climbing trees. But she swung from her strong little arms and landed on all fours in the soft grass. Then she picked herself up and looked eagerly about her.

She was at the back of the house. Before her lay a garden in which a bent old man was working. Beyond the garden a little path through an open field led up a steep hill. At the top of the hill, a lone pine tree stood on guard beside the huge rock. Pollyanna felt there was just one place in the world worth being—on top of that big rock.

She skipped by the bent old man and, a little out of breath, reached the path that ran through the open field. Then she began to climb. Already, however, she was thinking what a long, long way off that rock must be. And back at the window it had looked so near!

Fifteen minutes later the great clock in the hallway of the Harrington home struck six. At precisely the last stroke, Nancy rang the bell for supper.

One, two, three minutes passed. Miss Polly frowned and tapped the floor with her slipper. She rose to her feet, went into the hall, and looked upstairs, plainly impatient.

"Nancy," she said firmly, "my niece is late. No, you do not need to call her," she added severely. "I told her what time supper was. She may as well learn to be punctual. When she comes down, she may have bread and milk in the kitchen."

"Yes, ma'am." It was well, perhaps, that Miss Polly did not happen to be looking at Nancy's face just then.

Just after supper, Nancy crept up the back stairs to the attic room. "Bread and milk, indeed!—and when the poor lamb has only just cried herself to sleep!" She softly pushed open the door. The next moment she gave a frightened cry. "Where are you? Where have you gone?" She looked in the closet, under the bed, and even in the trunk. Then she flew downstairs and out to Old Tom in the garden.

"Mr. Tom, that blessed child's gone," she wailed. "She's vanished right up into Heaven where she come from, poor lamb!"

The old man straightened up. "Gone? Heaven?" he repeated, gazing at the sunset sky. Then he said with a slow grin, "Well, Nancy, it do look like as if she'd tried to get as near Heaven as she could." He pointed to a slender figure balanced on top of a huge rock.

"Well, she ain't goin' to Heaven that way tonight!" declared Nancy as she sped toward the path that led through the open field.

5. THE GAME

"For the land's sake, Miss Pollyanna, what a scare you did give me," panted Nancy, hurrying up to the big rock.

Pollyanna slid down. "Scare? Oh, I'm so sorry. But you mustn't ever get scared about me, Nancy. Father and the Ladies' Aid used to, till they found I always came back all right."

"But I didn't even see you go," cried Nancy. "I guess you flew right up through the roof."

Pollyanna skipped. "I did, almost. Only I flew down instead of up. I came down the tree."

Nancy stopped short. "You did—what?"

"Came down the tree, outside my window."

"My stars and stockings!" gasped Nancy. "I'd like to know what your aunt would say to that!"

"Would you? Well, I'll tell her so you can find out," promised the little girl.

"Mercy!" gasped Nancy. "No—no!"

"Why, you don't mean she'd care!" cried Pollyanna.

"No—er—yes—well, never mind. But, say, we better hurry. I've got to get the dishes done, you know. And you must be hungry, too. I'm afraid you'll have to have bread and milk in the kitchen with me. Your aunt didn't like it when you didn't come down to supper, you know."

"But I couldn't. I was up here."

"Yes, but she didn't know that!" observed Nancy. "I'm sorry about the bread and milk."

"Oh, I'm not. I'm glad."

"Glad! Why?"

"Why, I like bread and milk. And I'd like to eat with you. I don't see any trouble about being glad about that."

"You don't seem to see any trouble bein' glad about everythin'," said Nancy, choking a little as she remembered Pollyanna's brave attempts to like the bare little attic room.

Pollyanna laughed softly. "Well, that's the game, you know."

"The *game?*"

"Yes—the 'just being glad' game."

"Whatever in the world are you talkin' about?"

"Why, it's a game. Father told it to me, and it's lovely," explained Pollyanna. "We've played it always, ever since I was a little, little girl."

"What is it? I ain't much on games."

Pollyanna laughed again, but she sighed, too. In the twilight her face looked thin and wistful. "Why, we began it on some crutches that came in a missionary barrel."

"Crutches!"

"Yes. You see, I'd wanted a doll. But when the barrel came, the lady wrote that no dolls had come in, but the little crutches had. So she sent 'em along as they might come in handy for some child, sometime. And that's when we began the game."

"Well, I must say I can't see any game about that," declared Nancy.

"Oh, yes. The game was to just find something about everything to be glad about—no matter what," Pollyanna said earnestly. "And we began right then— on the crutches."

"Well, goodness me! I can't see anythin' to be glad about—gettin' a pair of crutches when you wanted a doll!"

Pollyanna clapped her hands. "There is! There is!" she crowed. "But I couldn't see it either, at first. Father had to tell it to me."

"Well, then, suppose you tell me," almost snapped Nancy.

"Why, just be glad because you *don't need 'em!*" cried Pollyanna. "You see, it's easy when you know how!"

"Well, of all the strange things!" breathed Nancy.

"Oh, but it isn't strange—it's lovely," said Pollyanna. "And we've played it ever since. And the harder it is, the more fun it is. Only—only sometimes it's almost too hard—like when your father goes to Heaven, and there isn't anybody but a Ladies' Aid left."

"Yes, or when you're put in a little room at the top of the house with nothin' in it."

Pollyanna sighed. "That was a hard one, at first," she admitted, "especially when I was so lonesome. I just didn't feel like playing the game, and I *had* wanted pretty things! Then I happened to think how I hated to see my freckles in the looking-glass, and I saw that lovely picture out the window, too. You see, when you're hunting for the glad things, you sort of forget the other kind. It's a lovely game. Father and I used to like it so much. I suppose, though, it—it'll be a little harder now, as long as I haven't anybody to play it with. Maybe Aunt Polly will play it, though," she added.

"My stars and stockings! HER!" breathed Nancy, behind her teeth. Then, aloud, she said, "See here, Miss Pollyanna, I ain't sayin' that I'll play it very well, and I ain't sayin' that I know how, anyway. But I'll play it with you, I will!"

"Oh, Nancy!" cried Pollyanna, giving her a hug. "That'll be splendid! Won't we have fun?"

"Er—maybe," said Nancy with doubt. "But you mustn't count too much on me, you know. I never was good at games. But I'm goin' to make a most awful try on this one," she finished as they entered the kitchen together.

Pollyanna ate her bread and milk with good appetite. Then, at Nancy's suggestion, she went into the sitting room, where her aunt sat reading. Miss Polly looked up coldly.

"Have you had your supper, Pollyanna?"

"Yes, Aunt Polly."

"I'm sorry, Pollyanna, that already I had to send you into the kitchen to eat bread and milk."

"But I was real glad you did it, Aunt Polly. I like bread and milk, and Nancy, too. You mustn't feel bad about that one bit."

Aunt Polly sat suddenly a little straighter in her chair. "Pollyanna, it's quite time you were in bed. Nancy will give you a candle. Be careful how you handle it. Breakfast will be at half-past seven. Good night."

Pollyanna came straight to her aunt's side and gave her an affectionate hug. "I've had such a beautiful time, so far," she sighed happily. "I know I'm going to just love living with you but then, I knew before I came. Good night," she called cheerfully as she ran from the room.

"Well, upon my soul!" exclaimed Miss Polly. "What a most extraordinary child! She's 'glad' I punished her. Well, upon my soul!"

Fifteen minutes later, in the attic room, a lonely little girl sobbed, "I know, father-among-the-angels, I'm not playing the game one bit now—not one bit. But I don't believe even you could find anything to be glad about sleeping all alone up here in the dark. If only I was near Nancy or Aunt Polly, or even a Ladies' Aider, it would be easier!"

Downstairs in the kitchen, Nancy jabbed her dishrag into the milk pitcher and muttered, "If playin' a silly-fool game about bein' glad you've got crutches when you want dolls is to be my way of bein' that rock o' refuge—why, I'm goin' to play it. I am, I am!"

6. A Question of Duty

It was nearly seven o'clock when Pollyanna awoke that first day after her arrival. The little room was cooler now, and the air blew in fresh and sweet. Outside, the birds were twittering, and Pollyanna flew to the window to talk to them. She saw that down in the garden her aunt was already out among the rosebushes.

Down the attic stairs sped Pollyanna, leaving both doors wide open. She ran through the hall, then bang through the front screen door and around to the garden.

Aunt Polly, with the bent old man, was leaning over a rose bush when Pollyanna flung herself upon her. "Oh, Aunt Polly, Aunt Polly, I reckon I am glad this morning just to be alive!"

"PollyANNA!" protested the lady sternly. "Is this the usual way you say good morning?"

The little girl dropped to her toes, and danced lightly up and down.

"No, only when I love folks so I just can't help it!"

Miss Polly attempted a frown—without her usual success. "Pollyanna, you—Thomas, that will do for this morning," she said stiffly. Then she turned and walked rapidly away.

"Do you always work in the garden, Mr.—Man?" asked Pollyanna with interest.

"Yes, Miss. I'm Old Tom, the gardener," he answered. Timidly, he reached out a shaking hand and let it rest for a moment on her bright hair. "You are so like your mother, little Miss! I used to know her when she was even littler than you be."

"You knew my mother, really? When she was just a little earth angel, and not a Heaven one? Oh, please tell me about her!"

A bell sounded from the house. The next moment Nancy flew out the back door.

"Miss Pollyanna, that bell means breakfast," she panted, pulling the little girl to her feet. "It means that you're to run like time when you hear it, no matter where you be." She rushed Pollyanna into the house as she would shoo an unruly chicken into a coop.

Breakfast, for the first five minutes, was a silent meal. Then Miss Polly saw two flies darting here and there over the table.

"Nancy," she said sternly, "where did those flies come from?"

"I don't know, ma'am. There wasn't one in the kitchen."

"I reckon maybe they're my flies, Aunt Polly," observed Pollyanna cheerfully. "There were lots of them this morning having a beautiful time upstairs."

"Yours!" gasped Miss Polly. "What do you mean? Where did they come from?"

"Why, Aunt Polly, they came from outside, through the windows. I saw some come in."

"You saw them! You mean you raised those windows without any screens?"

"Why, yes. There weren't any screens there, Aunt Polly."

"Nancy," directed Miss Polly, "go at once to Miss Pollyanna's room and shut the windows. Shut the doors, also. Later, when your morning work is done, go through every room with the flyswatter. See that you make a thorough search."

To her niece she said, "Pollyanna, I have ordered screens for those windows. I knew, of course, that it was my duty to do that. But it seems to me that you have quite forgotten your duty."

"My duty?" Pollyanna's eyes were wide with wonder.

"Certainly. I know it is warm, but I consider it your duty to keep your windows closed till those screens come. Flies, Pollyanna, are very dangerous to health. After breakfast I will give you a little pamphlet on this matter to read."

"To read? Oh, thank you, Aunt Polly. I love to read!"

Miss Polly drew in her breath, then she shut her lips together hard.

Pollyanna, seeing her stern face, said, "Of course I'm sorry about the duty I forgot, Aunt Polly. I won't raise the windows again."

Her aunt did not speak until the meal was over. Then she went to the bookcase in the sitting room, and took out a small paper booklet. "This is the article I spoke of, Pollyanna. Go to your room at once and read it. I will be up in half an hour to look over your things."

Pollyanna saw the illustration of a fly's head, many times magnified, and cried joyously, "Oh, thank you, Aunt Polly!" She skipped merrily from the room, banging the door behind her.

Half an hour later, Miss Polly, her face expressing stern duty in every line, climbed the attic stairs and entered Pollyanna's room. She was greeted with a burst of enthusiasm.

"Oh, Aunt Polly, I never saw anything so interesting in my life. I'm so glad you gave me that book to read! Why, I didn't suppose flies could carry such a lot of things on their feet, and—"

"That will do," observed Aunt Polly. "Pollyanna, you may bring out your clothes now, and I will look them over. What are not suitable for you I shall give away."

Pollyanna reluctantly laid down the pamphlet and turned toward the closet. "I'm afraid you'll think they're worse than the Ladies' Aid did," she sighed. "But there were mostly things for boys and older folks in the last barrels. Did you ever have a missionary barrel, Aunt Polly?"

At her aunt's look of shock, Pollyanna corrected herself at once.

"Why, no, of course you didn't, Aunt Polly!" she said with a blush. "I forgot. Rich folks never have to have them. But you see sometimes I kind of forget that you are rich—up here in this room, you know."

Miss Polly's lips parted, but no words came. Pollyanna, unaware that she had said anything unpleasant, hurried on.

"Well, you can't tell a thing about missionary barrels, except that you won't find in 'em what you think you're going to. It was the barrels that were hardest to play the game on, for father and—"

Just in time Pollyanna remembered that she was not to talk of her father to her aunt. She dived into her closet and brought out the poor little dresses.

With the tips of her fingers Miss Polly turned over the garments. Next she examined the patched undergarments in the bureau drawers.

"I've got the best ones on," confessed Pollyanna. "The Ladies' Aid bought me one set."

Miss Polly did not seem to hear. She turned to Pollyanna and asked abruptly, "You have been to school, of course, Pollyanna?"

"Oh, yes, Aunt Polly. Besides, fath—I mean, I was taught at home some, too."

Miss Polly frowned. "Very good. In the fall you will enter school here. Meanwhile, I suppose I ought to hear you read aloud half an hour each day. Have you studied music?"

"Not much. I learned to play on the piano a little. Miss Gray—she plays for church—she taught me. But I'd just as soon let that go, Aunt Polly."

"Very likely," observed Aunt Polly, with uplifted eyebrows. "Nevertheless I think it is my duty to see that you are properly instructed in music. You sew, of course."

"Yes, ma'am." Pollyanna sighed. "The Ladies' Aid taught me that. But I had an awful time. Mrs. Jones didn't believe in holding your needle like the rest of 'em did, and Mrs. White thought backstitching ought to be taught you before hemming—or else the other way."

"Well, I shall teach you sewing myself. You do not know how to cook, I presume."

Pollyanna laughed. "They were just beginning to teach me that this summer, but I hadn't got far. I'd only learned chocolate fudge and fig cake when—when I had to stop." Her voice broke.

"Chocolate fudge and fig cake, indeed!" scorned Miss Polly. "At nine o'clock every morning, you will read aloud one half-hour to me. Before that you will use the time to put this room in order. Wednesday and Saturday mornings, after half-past nine, you will spend with Nancy in the kitchen, learning to cook. Other mornings you will sew with me. That will leave the afternoons for your music."

Pollyanna cried out in dismay. "Oh, but Aunt Polly, you haven't left me any time at all just to—to *live*."

"To live, child! What do you mean?"

"I mean living—doing the things you want to do: playing outdoors, reading, climbing hills, talking to Mr. Tom in the garden, and Nancy, and finding out all about the houses and the people and everything everywhere all through the perfectly lovely streets I came through yesterday. That's what I call living, Aunt Polly."

Miss Polly lifted her head irritably. "Pollyanna, you *are* the most extraordinary child! You will be allowed a proper amount of playtime. But if I am willing to do my duty in seeing that you have proper care and instruction, you ought to be willing to do yours by seeing that that care and instruction are not ungratefully wasted."

Pollyanna looked shocked. "Oh, Aunt Polly, as if I ever could be ungrateful—to you! Why, I love you—and you aren't even a Ladies' Aider!"

"Very well, then. See that you don't act ungrateful," said Miss Polly as she turned toward the door. She had gone halfway down the stairs when a small, unsteady voice called after her.

"Please, Aunt Polly, you didn't tell me which of my things you wanted to—to give away."

Aunt Polly gave a tired sigh. "Not one of your garments is fit for my niece to wear. Certainly I would be far from doing my duty by you if I let you appear in any one of them."

Pollyanna sighed now. She believed she was going to hate that word, *duty.* "Aunt Polly, please," she called, "isn't there any way you can be glad about all that *duty* business?"

"What?" Miss Polly looked up in dazed surprise. Then, suddenly, with very red cheeks, she turned and swept angrily down the stairs. "Don't be impertinent, Pollyanna!"

In the hot little attic room Pollyanna dropped onto one of the straight-backed chairs.

For several minutes she sat in silence, her eyes fixed on the forlorn heap of garments on the bed. Then, slowly, she rose and began to put away the dresses. "There just isn't anything to be glad about, that I can see," she said aloud. "Unless it's to be glad when the duty's done!" she laughed.

7. POLLYANNA AND PUNISHMENTS

At half-past one o'clock, Timothy drove Miss Polly and her niece to four or five stores to buy a new wardrobe for Pollyanna.

Miss Polly came out of it with the feeling one might have at finding oneself at last on solid earth after a perilous walk across the very thin crust of a volcano. Pollyanna herself came out of it with radiant smiles. As she told one of the clerks, "When you haven't had anybody but missionary barrels and Ladies' Aiders to dress you, it's perfectly lovely to just walk right in and buy clothes that are brand-new, and that don't have to be tucked up or let down because they don't fit!"

The shopping trip took up the entire afternoon. Then came supper and a delightful talk with Old Tom in the garden, and another with Nancy on the back porch. Old Tom told Pollyanna wonderful things of her mother, which made her very happy indeed. Nancy told her all about the little farm six miles away at "The Corners," where lived her own dear mother, and her brother and sisters. She promised, too, that sometime she would take Pollyanna to see them.

"And they've got lovely names, too," sighed Nancy. "They're 'Algernon,' and 'Florabelle' and 'Estelle.' I—I just hate 'Nancy'!"

"But I love 'Nancy,' just because it's you," declared Pollyanna. "And anyhow," she chuckled, "you can be glad it isn't 'Hephzibah.'"

"Hephzibah!"

"Yes. In the Ladies' Aid, Mrs. White's name is that. Her husband calls her 'Hep,' and she doesn't like it. She says when he calls out 'Hep—Hep!' she feels as if the next minute he was going to yell 'Hurrah!'"

Nancy smiled. "Well, I'll never hear 'Nancy' again without thinking of 'Hep—Hep!' My, I guess I *am* glad—" She stopped short and turned amazed eyes on the little girl. "Say, Miss Pollyanna, was you playin' that game then?"

Pollyanna frowned, then laughed. "Why, Nancy, that's so! I *was* playing the game. But I just did it without thinking. You get so used to looking for something to be glad about, you know. And generally there is something about everything that you can be glad about, if you keep hunting long enough to find it."

"Well, maybe," said Nancy, with doubt.

At half-past eight Pollyanna went up to bed. The screens had not yet come, and the little room was like an oven. With longing eyes Pollyanna looked at the two closed windows. But she did not raise them. She undressed, folded her clothes neatly, said her prayers, blew out her candle, and climbed into bed.

She lay in sleepless misery, tossing from side to side of the hot little cot. Finally she slipped out of bed, felt her way across the room, and opened her door. Out in the main attic, all was velvet blackness except where the moon flung a path of silver across the floor from the east dormer window. Pollyanna drew a quick breath and pattered straight into that silvery path, and on to the window. Outside, there was fresh, sweet air that would feel so good to hot cheeks and hands!

As she peered out, she saw, only a little way below the window, the wide, flat tin roof of Miss Polly's sun parlor. If only her bed were out there in the cool, sweet night air!

Suddenly Pollyanna remembered that she had seen near this attic window a row of long white bags hanging from nails. Nancy had said that they contained the winter clothing, put away for the summer. Pollyanna felt her way to these bags. She selected a nice fat soft one for a bed, and a thinner one for a pillow. In high glee, she pattered to the moonlit window again, raised the sash, and pushed the bags through to the roof below. Then she let herself down, closing the window carefully behind her. She had not forgotten those flies with the marvelous feet that carried things.

How deliciously cool it was! Pollyanna danced with delight, drawing in long, full breaths of the refreshing air. She walked back and forth from end to end of the tin roof. It gave her such a pleasant sensation of airy space after her hot little room. And the roof was so broad and flat that she had no fear of falling off. Finally, she curled herself up and settled herself to sleep.

"I'm so glad now that the screens didn't come," she murmured, blinking up at the stars, "else I couldn't have had this!"

Downstairs, Miss Polly herself was hurrying into dressing gown and slippers, her face white and frightened. A minute before she had telephoned in a shaking voice to Timothy, "Come up quick—you and your father! Bring lanterns. Somebody is on the roof of the sun parlor. Hurry!"

Some time later, Pollyanna, just dropping off to sleep, was startled by a lantern flash. She opened her eyes to find Timothy at the top of a ladder near her, Old Tom just getting through the window, and her aunt peering out at her from behind him.

"Pollyanna, what does this mean?" cried Aunt Polly.

Pollyanna blinked sleepy eyes and sat up. "Why, Mr. Tom—Aunt Polly!" she stammered. "Don't look so scared! It's only that I was so hot in there. But I shut the window, Aunt Polly, so the flies couldn't carry those germ-things in."

Miss Polly bit her lip hard, then she said sternly, "Pollyanna, hand those things to me at once and come in here. Of all the extraordinary children!"

To Pollyanna the air in the attic was all the more stifling after that cool breath of outdoors. But she did not complain. She only drew a long sigh.

At the top of the stairs Miss Polly jerked out crisply, "For the rest of the night, Pollyanna, you are to sleep in my bed with me. The screens will be here tomorrow, but until then I consider it my duty to keep you where I know where you are."

"With you?—in your bed?" Pollyanna cried. "Oh, Aunt Polly, how perfectly lovely of you! My! I am glad now those screens didn't come!"

Miss Polly was stalking on ahead. Miss Polly, to tell the truth, was feeling helpless. For the third time since Pollyanna's arrival, Miss Polly was punishing Pollyanna— and for the third time she faced the amazing fact that Pollyanna took her punishment as a special reward.

8. Pollyanna Pays a Visit

Life at the Harrington home settled into something like order, though not exactly the order that Miss Polly had planned. Pollyanna sewed, practiced, read aloud, and studied cooking in the kitchen. But she also had time to "just live." Every afternoon from two until six o'clock was hers to do as she liked, provided she did not "like" to do certain things prohibited by Aunt Polly.

Almost every pleasant afternoon Pollyanna begged for an errand to run, so that she might walk in one direction or another. It was on these walks that she often met the Man.

The Man often wore a long black coat and a high silk hat. His face was clean-shaven and pale, and his hair, below his hat, was somewhat gray. He walked rapidly, and he was always alone, which made Pollyanna sorry for him. Perhaps it was because of this that she one day spoke to him.

"How do you do, sir? Isn't this a nice day?" she called cheerily.

The man threw a hurried glance about him, then stopped. "Did you speak to me?" he asked in a sharp voice.

"Yes, sir," beamed Pollyanna. "I say, it's a nice day, isn't it?"

"Humph!" he grunted, and strode on again.

Pollyanna laughed. He was such a funny man, she thought. The next day she saw him again.

"It isn't quite so nice as yesterday, but it's pretty nice," she called out cheerfully.

"Eh? Humph!" grunted the man as before, and once again Pollyanna laughed.

The third time Pollyanna greeted him in the same manner, the man stopped abruptly.

"See here, child, who are you, and why are you speaking to me every day?"

"I'm Pollyanna Whittier, and I thought you looked lonesome. I'm so glad you stopped. Now we're introduced, only I don't know your name yet."

"Well, of all the—" The man did not finish his sentence, but strode on faster than ever.

Pollyanna looked after him with a disappointed droop to her usually smiling lips. "Maybe he didn't understand—but that was only half an introduction. I don't know his name yet."

Pollyanna was carrying jelly to Mrs. Snow today. Miss Polly Harrington always sent something to Mrs. Snow once a week. She said she thought that it was her duty, since Mrs. Snow was poor, sick, and a member of her church. Today Pollyanna had begged to go in Nancy's place.

"I'd love to do it, Nancy."

"Well, you won't after you've done it once," predicted Nancy sourly.

"Why not?"

"Because if folks wasn't sorry for her, not a soul would go near her from mornin' till night. She's that cantankerous. I pity her daughter. She *has* to take care of her."

"But, why, Nancy?"

"Well, nothin' is right in Mrs. Snow's eyes. If it's Monday, she's bound to say she wished it was Sunday. And if you take her jelly you're pretty sure to hear she wanted chicken. But if you did bring her chicken, she'd ask for lamb broth!"

"Why, what a funny woman," laughed Pollyanna. "I think I shall like to go to see her. She must be so surprising and—and different. I love *different* folks."

"Humph! Well, Mrs. Snow's 'different,' all right!" Nancy finished grimly.

Pollyanna was thinking of these remarks as she turned in at the gate of the shabby little cottage. Her eyes sparkled at the thought of meeting this "different" Mrs. Snow.

A pale-faced, tired-looking young girl answered her knock at the door.

"How do you do?" began Pollyanna politely. "I'm from Miss Polly Harrington, and I'd like to see Mrs. Snow, please."

The girl turned and led the way through the hall to a door at the end of it. In the sickroom, Pollyanna blinked a little before she could see in the gloom. Then she saw a woman half-sitting up in the bed across the room.

"How do you do, Mrs. Snow? Aunt Polly says she hopes you are comfortable today, and she's sent you some jelly."

"Dear me! Jelly?" murmured a fretful voice. "Of course I'm very much obliged, but I was hoping it would be lamb broth today."

Pollyanna frowned a little. "Why, I thought it was chicken you wanted when folks brought you jelly," she said.

"What?" The sick woman turned sharply.

"Why, nothing," apologized Pollyanna. "It's only that Nancy said it was chicken you wanted when we brought jelly, and lamb broth when we brought chicken. But maybe it was the other way, and Nancy forgot."

The sick woman sat straight up in the bed—a most unusual thing for her to do, though Pollyanna did not know this.

"Well, Miss Impertinence, who are you?" she demanded.

Pollyanna laughed gleefully. "Oh, that isn't my name, Mrs. Snow—and I'm glad it isn't, too! I'm Pollyanna Whittier, Miss Polly Harrington's niece, and I've come to live with her. That's why I'm here with the jelly this morning."

The sick woman fell back on her pillow listlessly.

"Your aunt is very kind, of course, but my appetite isn't very good this morning, and I was wanting lamb—" She stopped suddenly, then said, "I never slept a wink last night—not a wink!"

"O dear, I wish I didn't," sighed Pollyanna, placing the jelly on the little stand and seating herself in the nearest chair. "You lose such a lot of time just sleeping! Don't you think so?"

"Lose time—sleeping!" exclaimed the sick woman.

"Yes, when you might be just living, you know. It seems a pity we can't live nights, too."

Once again the woman sat up in her bed. "Well, if you ain't amazing!" she cried. "Go to that window and pull up the curtain," she directed. "I should like to know what you look like!"

"Oh dear! Then you'll see my freckles, won't you?" Pollyanna sighed as she went to the window. "And just when I was so glad it was dark and you couldn't see 'em. There! Now you can—oh!" she broke off as she turned back to the bed. "I'm so glad you wanted to see me, because now I can see you! They didn't tell me you were so pretty!"

"Me! Pretty!" scoffed the woman.

"Why, yes. Didn't you know it?" cried Pollyanna.

"Well, no, I didn't," retorted Mrs. Snow. For fifteen years she had been too busy wishing things were different to find much time to enjoy things as they were.

"Oh, but your eyes are so big and dark, and your hair's all dark, too, and curly," cooed Pollyanna. "And you've got two little red spots in your cheeks. Why, Mrs. Snow, you *are* pretty! Just let me show you." She skipped over to the bureau and picked up a small hand mirror.

On the way back to the bed she stopped. "If you don't mind, I'd like to fix your hair just a little before I let you see it," she proposed. "May I fix your hair, please?"

"Why, I—suppose so, if you want to," permitted Mrs. Snow, grudgingly.

"Oh, thank you. I love to fix people's hair," cried Pollyanna, reaching for a comb. "I won't do much today, of course. I'm in such a hurry for you to see how pretty you are. But some day I'm going to take it all down and have a perfectly lovely time with it!"

For five minutes Pollyanna worked swiftly. Meanwhile the sick woman was, in spite of herself, beginning to tingle with a feeling near to excitement.

"There!" said Pollyanna, hastily plucking a carnation from a nearby vase and tucking it into the dark hair. "Now I reckon we're ready to be looked at!"

"Humph!" grunted the sick woman, eyeing her reflection severely. "It won't last, with me tossing back and forth on the pillow as I do."

"Of course not—and I'm glad, too," nodded Pollyanna, "because then I can fix it again. Anyhow, I should think you'd be glad it's black—black shows up so much nicer on a pillow than yellow hair like mine does."

Mrs. Snow dropped the mirror and turned irritably. "Well, you wouldn't be glad for black hair nor anything else if you had to lie here all day as I do!"

Pollyanna bent her brows in a thoughtful frown.

"Why, it would be kind of hard to do it then, wouldn't it?" she mused aloud.

"Do what?"

"Be glad about things."

"Be glad about things? When you're sick in bed all your days? Well, I should say it would," retorted Mrs. Snow. "If you don't think so, just tell me something to be glad about!"

To Mrs. Snow's amazement, Pollyanna sprang to her feet and clapped her hands. "Oh, good! That'll be a hard one, won't it? I've got to go, now, but I'll think and think all the way home. And maybe the next time I come I can tell it to you. Good-bye. I've had a lovely time! Good-bye," she called again, as she skipped through the doorway.

"Well, I never! Now, what does she mean by that?" cried Mrs. Snow.

By and by she turned her head and picked up the mirror. "That little thing has got a knack with hair," she muttered. "I declare, I didn't know it could look so pretty. But then, what's the use?" she sighed.

9. WHICH TELLS OF THE MAN

It rained the next time Pollyanna saw the Man. She greeted him, however, with a bright smile. "It isn't so nice today, is it?" she called. "I'm glad it doesn't rain always, anyhow!"

The man did not even grunt this time, nor turn his head. Pollyanna decided that he did not hear her. Therefore, on the following day, she spoke up louder.

"How do you do?" she chirped. "I'm so glad it isn't yesterday, aren't you?"

The man stopped with a scowl on his face. "See here, little girl, we might just as well settle this thing right now," he began. "I've got something besides the weather to think of. I don't know whether the sun shines or not."

"No, sir, I thought you didn't. That's why I told you—so you would notice it—that the sun shines, and all that. I knew you'd be glad it did if you only stopped to think of it."

"See here," said the man, "why don't you find someone your own age to talk to?"

"I'd like to, sir, but there aren't any 'round here. Still, I don't mind so very much. I like old folks just as well, maybe better, sometimes—being used to the Ladies' Aid, so."

"Humph! The Ladies' Aid, indeed! Is that what you took me for?" The man's lips were threatening to smile, but the scowl above them was still stern.

Pollyanna laughed. "Oh, no, sir. You don't look a mite like a Ladies' Aider. I'm sure you're much nicer than you look!"

"Well, of all the—" he said as he turned and strode on as before.

The next time Pollyanna met the Man, his eyes were gazing straight into hers.

"Good afternoon," he greeted her a little stiffly. "Perhaps I'd better say right away that I *know* the sun is shining today."

"But you don't have to tell me," said Pollyanna. "I knew it just as soon as I saw you."

"Oh, you did, did you?"

"Yes, sir. I saw it in your eyes, you know, and in your smile."

"Humph!" grunted the man, as he passed on.

The Man always spoke to Pollyanna after this, though usually he said little but "good afternoon." Even that, however, was a great surprise to Nancy, who chanced to be with Pollyanna one day when they met the Man.

"Sakes alive, Miss Pollyanna," she gasped, "did that man speak to you?"

"Why, yes, he always does—now," smiled Pollyanna.

"Goodness! Do you know who he is?" demanded Nancy.

Pollyanna frowned and shook her head.

"I reckon he forgot to tell me. I did my part of the introducing, but he didn't."

Nancy's eyes widened. "But he never speaks to anybody, child. He hasn't for years, except when he just has to, for business. He's John Pendleton. He lives all by himself in the big house on Pendleton Hill. He's got loads of money, John Pendleton has—from his father. There ain't nobody in town as rich as he is. He could eat dollar bills, if he wanted to. Some says he's crazy, and some just cross. And some says he's got a skeleton in his closet."

"Oh, Nancy!" shuddered Pollyanna. "How can he keep such a dreadful thing? I should think he'd throw it away!"

Nancy chuckled. That Pollyanna had taken the skeleton literally instead of figuratively, she knew very well. But she did not correct the mistake.

"Everybody says he's mysterious," she went on. "Some years he just travels, week in and week out, in Egypt and Asia and the Desert of Sarah, you know. When he comes back he writes books—odd books, they say, about some gimcrack he's found in those countries."

"He is a funny man," declared Pollyanna, "and he's different, too, just like Mrs. Snow, only he's a different different."

"Well, I guess he is," chuckled Nancy.

"I'm gladder than ever now, anyhow, that he speaks to me," said Pollyanna.

10. A Surprise for Mrs. Snow

The next time Pollyanna went to see Mrs. Snow, she found her again in a darkened room.

"Oh, it's you, is it?" asked a fretful voice from the bed. "I remember you. I wish you had come yesterday."

"Do you? Well, I'm glad it isn't any farther away from yesterday than today is," laughed Pollyanna, setting her basket carefully down on a chair. "My! but aren't you dark here, though? I can't see you a bit," she cried, crossing to the window and pulling up the shade. "I want to see if you've fixed your hair like I did—oh, you haven't! But never mind. Now I want you to see what I've brought you."

The woman turned her eyes toward the basket. "Well, what is it?"

"Guess! What do you want?"

The sick woman frowned. "Why, I don't want anything, as I know of," she sighed. "After all, they all taste alike!"

Pollyanna chuckled. "This won't. Guess! If you did want something, what would it be?"

The woman hesitated. "Well, of course, there's lamb broth—"

"I've got it!" crowed Pollyanna.

"But that's what I didn't want," sighed the sick woman, sure now of what her stomach craved. "It was chicken I wanted."

"Oh, I've got that, too," chuckled Pollyanna.

The woman turned in amazement. "Both of them?" she demanded.

"Yes—and jelly," exclaimed Pollyanna. "I was determined you should have what you wanted for once. So, Nancy and I fixed it. Oh, of course, there's only a little of each—but there's some of all of 'em! I'm so glad you did want chicken," she went on as she lifted the three little bowls from her basket. "You see, I got to thinking on the way here—what if you should say onions, or something like that, that I didn't have! Wouldn't it have been a shame when I'd tried so hard?" she laughed merrily.

There was no reply.

Pollyanna arranged the three bowls on the table. "How do you do today?" she asked.

"Very poorly, thank you," murmured Mrs. Snow. "I lost my nap this morning. Nellie Higgins next door has begun music lessons, and her practicing drives me nearly wild. She was at it all the morning—every minute! I'm sure I don't know what I shall do!"

Pollyanna nodded sympathetically.

"I know. It is awful! Mrs. White had it once—one of my Ladies' Aiders, you know. She told me she reckoned she'd have gone crazy if it hadn't been for Mr. White's sister's ears."

"Sister's *ears!* What do you mean?"

Pollyanna laughed. "You see, Miss White was deaf—awfully deaf. And she came to visit 'em. After that, every time the piano started to play across the street, Mrs. White felt so glad she could hear it, that she didn't mind so much that she *did* hear it. You see, she was playing the game, too. I'd told her about it."

"The game?"

Pollyanna clapped her hands.

"There! I almost forgot. I've thought it up, Mrs. Snow—what you can be glad about."

"Glad about! What do you mean?"

"Why, I told you I would. Don't you remember? You asked me to tell you something to be glad about even though you did have to lie here in bed all day."

"Oh!" scoffed the woman. "Yes, I remember that. But I didn't suppose you meant it."

"Oh, yes, I did," nodded Pollyanna. "And I found it, too."

"Did you really? Well, what is it?" Mrs. Snow's voice was sarcastically polite.

Pollyanna drew a long breath. "I thought how glad you could be that other folks weren't like you—all sick in bed like this, you know."

Mrs. Snow stared. Her eyes were angry. "Well, really!"

"And now I'll tell you the game," proposed Pollyanna. "It'll be just lovely for you to play—it'll be so hard. And there's so much more fun when it is hard! You see, it's like this." And she began to tell of the missionary barrel, the crutches, and the doll that did not come.

The story was just finished when Milly appeared at the door. "Your aunt wants you, Miss Pollyanna," she said. "She says you're to hurry."

Pollyanna rose reluctantly. "All right," she sighed. "I'll hurry." Suddenly she laughed. "I suppose I ought to be glad I've got legs to hurry with, hadn't I, Mrs. Snow?"

There was no answer. Mrs. Snow's eyes were closed. But Milly, whose eyes were wide open with surprise, saw that there were tears on her cheeks.

One by one the July days passed. To Pollyanna, they were happy days, indeed.

One afternoon Pollyanna came down from her attic room and met her aunt on the stairway. "Why, Aunt Polly, how perfectly lovely!" she cried. "You were coming up to see me! Come right in. I love company." She scampered up the stairs and threw her door wide open.

Now Miss Polly had not planned to call on her niece. She had been planning to look for a white wool shawl in the cedar chest. But to her surprise, she found herself in Pollyanna's little room sitting in one of the straight-backed chairs.

"I love company," said Pollyanna again. "And of course now I just love this room, even if it hasn't got the carpets and curtains and pictures that I'd been want—" With a blush Pollyanna stopped short.

"What's that, Pollyanna?"

"N-nothing, Aunt Polly, truly. I didn't mean to say it."

"Probably not," said Miss Polly, coldly. "But you did say it, so suppose we have the rest."

"But it wasn't anything, only that I'd been planning on pretty carpets and lace curtains and things, you know. But, I shouldn't have, of course, Aunt Polly," she apologized. "It was only because I'd always wanted them and hadn't had them, I suppose. Oh, we'd had two rugs in the barrels, but they were little, and one had ink spots, and the other holes. And there were only those two pictures: the one fath—I mean the good one we sold, and the bad one that broke. But, truly, Aunt Polly, there couldn't be a nicer picture than the one out my window there, and you've been so good to me, that—"

Miss Polly rose suddenly to her feet. Her face was very red. "That will do, Pollyanna," she said stiffly. "You have said quite enough, I'm sure."

Less than twenty-four hours later, Miss Polly said to Nancy crisply, "Nancy, you may move Miss Pollyanna's things downstairs this morning to the room directly beneath. I have decided to have my niece sleep there for the present."

"Yes, ma'am," said Nancy. To Pollyanna, a minute later, she cried joyously, "Just listen to this, Miss Pollyanna. You're to sleep downstairs in the room straight under this. You are, you are!"

Pollyanna flew downstairs two steps at a time. Bang went two doors and a chair before Pollyanna at last reached Aunt Polly. "Oh, Aunt Polly, Aunt Polly, did you mean it, really? Why, that room's got *everything*—the carpet and curtains and three pictures. Oh, Aunt Polly!"

"Very well, Pollyanna. I trust you will take proper care of them. And Pollyanna, please pick up that chair; and, you have banged two doors in the last half-minute."

Pollyanna picked up the chair. "I know I banged those doors," she admitted cheerfully. "You see, I'd just found out about the room, and I reckon you'd have banged doors if—" Pollyanna stopped short and eyed her aunt with new interest. "Aunt Polly, did you ever bang doors?"

"I hope not, Pollyanna!" Miss Polly's voice was shocked.

"Why, Aunt Polly, what a shame!"

"A shame!" repeated Aunt Polly.

"Why, yes. You see, if you'd felt like banging doors you'd have banged 'em, of course. And if you didn't, that must have meant that you weren't ever glad over anything—or you would have banged 'em. You couldn't have helped it. And I'm so sorry you weren't ever glad over anything!"

"Pollyanna!" gasped the lady. But Pollyanna was gone, and only the distant bang of the attic-stairway door answered for her.

11. Introducing Jimmy

August brought several surprises and some changes.

First there was the kitten. Pollyanna found the kitten mewing pitifully some distance down the road. When none of the neighbors claimed it, Pollyanna brought it home at once.

"And I was glad I didn't find anyone who owned it," she told her aunt. "I did so want to bring it home all the time. I love kitties. I knew you'd be glad to let it live here."

Miss Polly looked at the forlorn little gray bunch of misery in Pollyanna's arms, and shivered. Miss Polly did not care for cats—not even pretty, healthy, clean ones. "Ugh! What a dirty little beast! And it's sick, I'm sure, and all mangy."

"I know it, poor little thing," crooned Pollyanna tenderly. "And it's all trembly, too, it's so scared. You see it doesn't know, yet, that we're going to keep it. Of course I knew that you wouldn't let a dear little lonesome kitty go hunting for a home when you'd just taken me in. Why, I had the Ladies' Aid, and kitty didn't have anybody."

"But, Pollyanna…" protested Miss Polly. "I don't—"

But Pollyanna was already halfway to the kitchen, calling, "Nancy, Nancy, just see this dear little kitty that Aunt Polly is going to bring up along with me!"

The next day it was a dog, even dirtier and more forlorn than the kitten. And again Miss Polly, to her amazement, found herself in the role of a kind protector and an angel of mercy.

In less than a week, however, when Pollyanna brought home a small, ragged boy, and claimed the same protection for him, Miss Polly did have something to say. It happened this way.

On a pleasant Thursday morning Pollyanna had been taking jelly again to Mrs. Snow. Mrs. Snow and Pollyanna were the best of friends now. Mrs. Snow herself was playing the game with Pollyanna. To be sure, she was not playing it very well. She had been sorry for everything for so long, that it was not easy to be glad for anything now. But she was learning fast.

Pollyanna was thinking of this now when suddenly she saw the boy. He was sitting in a sad little heap by the roadside, whittling a small stick.

"Hullo," smiled Pollyanna.

The boy glanced up, but he looked away again, at once. "Hullo yourself," he mumbled.

Pollyanna laughed. "My name's Pollyanna Whittier," she began pleasantly. "What's yours?"

"Jimmy Bean," he grunted.

"Good! Now we're introduced. I'm glad you did your part. Some folks don't, you know. I live at Miss Polly Harrington's house. Where do you live?"

"Nowhere."

"Nowhere! Why, you can't do that—everybody lives somewhere," said Pollyanna.

"Well, I don't—just now. I'm huntin' up a new place."

"Oh! Where is it?"

The boy regarded her with scornful eyes. "Silly! As if I'd be a-huntin' for it—if I knew!"

Pollyanna did not like to be called "silly." "Where did you live—before?" she asked.

The boy looked a little pleasanter when he spoke this time.

"All right then—here goes! I'm Jimmy Bean, and I'm ten years old goin' on eleven. I come last year to live at the Orphans' Home. But they've got so many kids there ain't much room for me, an' I was never wanted, anyhow. So I've quit. I'm goin' to live somewheres else—but I haven't found the place, yet. I'd like a home—just a common one, you know, with a mother in it. I've tried four houses, but they didn't want me—though I said I expected to work, of course. There! Is that all you want to know?" The boy's voice had broken a little over the last two sentences.

"Why, what a shame!" cried Pollyanna. "And didn't there anybody want you? Oh dear! I know just how you feel, because after—after my father died, there wasn't anybody but the Ladies' Aid for me, until Aunt Polly said she'd take—" Pollyanna stopped abruptly.

"Oh, I know just the place for you!" she cried. "Aunt Polly'll take you—I know she will! Didn't she take me? And didn't she take Fluffy and Buffy, when they didn't have anyone to love them, or any place to go? And they're only cats and dogs. Oh, come, I know Aunt Polly'll take you! You don't know how good and kind she is!"

Jimmy Bean's thin little face brightened. "Honest? Would she, now? I'd work, you know, and I'm real strong!" He bared a small, bony arm.

"Of course she would! Why, my Aunt Polly is the nicest lady in the world—now that my mama has gone to be a Heaven angel. And there's rooms—heaps of 'em. It's an awful big house. It's perfectly lovely! Maybe she'll let you read the book about flies if you're good—I mean, if you're bad."

When they reached the house, Pollyanna steered her companion straight into the presence of her amazed aunt.

"Oh, Aunt Polly, just look here! I've got something ever so much nicer than Fluffy and Buffy for you to bring up. It's a real live boy. He won't mind a bit sleeping in the attic, and he says he'll work. But I shall need him most of the time to play with, I reckon."

Miss Polly grew white, then very red. "Pollyanna, what does this mean? Who is this dirty little boy? Where did you find him?" she demanded sharply.

The "dirty little boy" fell back a step and looked toward the door. Pollyanna laughed. "There, if I didn't forget to tell you his name! I'm as bad as the Man. And he is dirty, too, isn't he?—I mean, the boy is—just like Fluffy and Buffy were when you took them in. But he'll improve all right by washing, just as they did, and—oh, I almost forgot again," she broke off with a laugh. "This is Jimmy Bean, Aunt Polly."

"Well, what is he doing here?"

"Why, Aunt Polly, I just told you!" Pollyanna's eyes were wide with surprise. "He's for you. I brought him home—so he could live here, you know. He wants a home and folks. I told him how good you were to me, and to Fluffy and Buffy, and that I knew you would be to him, because of course he's even nicer than cats and dogs."

Miss Polly dropped back in her chair. "That will do, Pollyanna. This is the most absurd thing you've done yet. As if tramp cats and mangy dogs weren't bad enough but you must bring home ragged little beggars from the street, who—"

There was a sudden stir from the boy. His eyes flashed and his chin came up. He confronted Miss Polly fearlessly.

"I ain't a beggar. I was going to work, of course, for my board and keep. I wouldn't have come to your old house, anyhow, if this girl hadn't made me, a-tellin' me how you was so good and kind that you'd be just dyin' to take me in. So, there!" And he stalked from the room.

"Oh, Aunt Polly," choked Pollyanna. "Why, I thought you'd be *glad* to have him here! I'm sure, I should think you'd be glad—"

Miss Polly's nerves snapped at last. "Pollyanna," she cried sharply, *"will* you stop using that word *glad*! It's *glad— glad—glad* from morning till night until I think I shall grow wild!"

Pollyanna's jaw dropped. "Why, Aunt Polly," she breathed, "I should think you'd be glad to have me gl—Oh!" she broke off, clapping her hand to her lips and hurrying from the room.

Before the boy had reached the end of the driveway, Pollyanna overtook him.

"Boy! Boy! Jimmy Bean, I want you to know how—how sorry I am," she panted.

"Sorry nothin'! I ain't blamin' you," replied the boy. "But I ain't no beggar!"

"Of course you aren't! But you mustn't blame auntie. She is good and kind, really. But I probably didn't explain it right. I do wish I could find some place for you, though!"

The boy shrugged his shoulders and turned away. "Never mind. I can find one myself. I ain't no beggar, you know."

In the sitting-room window at that moment, Miss Polly watched the boy until a bend of the road hid him from sight. Then she sighed, turned, and walked slowly upstairs. In her ears still was the boy's scornful "you was so good and kind."

12. IN PENDLETON WOODS

Pollyanna was sure that nothing would do her so much good as a walk through the green quiet of Pendleton Woods. And so she climbed up Pendleton Hill, with the warm sun on her back.

It was always very beautiful in the Pendleton Woods. But today it seemed even more delightful than ever, despite her disappointment over Jimmy Bean.

Suddenly Pollyanna lifted her head and listened. A dog had barked in the distance. A moment later he came dashing toward her, still barking.

"Hullo, doggie—hullo!" Pollyanna looked down the path. She had seen the dog once before with the Man, Mr. John Pendleton. For some minutes she watched eagerly, but he did not appear. Then she turned her attention toward the dog.

The dog, as even Pollyanna could see, was acting strangely. He was still barking, giving little short, sharp yelps. He was running back and forth, too, in the path ahead.

Soon they reached a side path. Down this the little dog fairly flew, only to come back at once, whining and barking.

"Ho! That isn't the way home," laughed Pollyanna, still keeping to the main path.

The little dog seemed frantic now. Back and forth he ran, barking and whining pitifully. At last Pollyanna understood. She turned, and followed him.

Straight ahead, now, the little dog dashed. It was not long before Pollyanna came upon the reason for it all. There was a man lying motionless at the foot of a steep rock a few yards from the path.

A twig cracked sharply under Pollyanna's foot, and the man turned his head. Pollyanna ran to his side. "Mr. Pendleton! Oh, are you hurt?"

"Hurt? Oh, no! I'm just taking a siesta in the sunshine," snapped the man. "See here, how much do you know? What can you do? Have you got any sense?"

Pollyanna caught her breath with a little gasp. "Why, Mr. Pendleton, I—I don't know so very much, and I can't do a great many things. But most of the Ladies' Aiders said I had real good sense. I heard 'em say so one day—they didn't know I heard, though."

The man smiled grimly. "There, there, child, I beg your pardon. It's this confounded leg of mine. Now listen." He reached his hand into his trousers pocket and brought out a bunch of keys. "Straight through the path there, about five minutes' walk, is my house. This key will admit you to the side door. When you get into the house, go straight through the hall to the door at the end. On the big desk in the middle of the room you'll find a telephone. Do you know how to use a telephone?"

"Oh, yes, sir! Why, once—"

"Never mind," cut in the man. "Find Dr. Thomas Chilton's number on the card you'll see somewhere around there. Tell Dr. Chilton that John Pendleton is at the foot of Little Eagle Ledge in Pendleton Woods with a broken leg, and to come at once with a stretcher and two men."

"A broken leg? Oh, Mr. Pendleton, how perfectly awful!" And, with a little sobbing cry, Pollyanna went. She did not stop now to look up at the patches of blue between the sunlit tops of the trees. She kept her eyes on the ground to make sure that no twig nor stone tripped her hurrying feet.

It was not long before she came in sight of the house. She was almost frightened at the great pile of gray stone. She sped across the big neglected lawn and around the house to the side door. Her fingers, stiff from their tight clutch upon the keys, fumbled in their efforts to turn the bolt in the lock. But at last the heavy, carved door swung slowly back on its hinges.

Pollyanna paused a moment and looked fearfully around, her thoughts in a whirl. This was John Pendleton's house, the house of mystery, the house into which no one but its master entered—the house that sheltered, somewhere—a skeleton. With a little cry, Pollyanna ran through the hall to the door at the end and opened it. The room was large and dark. But through the west window, the sun threw a long shaft of gold across the telephone on the great desk in the middle of the room.

Pollyanna found the telephone card and ran her shaking forefinger down through the C's to "Chilton." Soon she had Dr. Chilton himself on the line, and was tremblingly delivering her message and answering the doctor's questions. Then she hung up and drew a long breath of relief.

Pollyanna glanced about her. She saw book-lined walls, a littered floor, an untidy desk, countless closed doors (any one of which might conceal a skeleton), and everywhere dust, dust, dust. She fled back through the hall to the great carved door, still half open as she had left it. In a short time, she was back in the woods at the man's side.

"Well, what is the trouble? Couldn't you get in?" he demanded.

"Why, of course I could!" she answered. "The doctor said he knew just where you were, so I didn't stay to show him. I wanted to be with you."

"Did you? Well, I can't say I admire your taste. I should think you might find more pleasant companions."

"Do you mean because you're so—cross?"

"Thanks for your frankness. Yes."

Pollyanna laughed softly. "But you're only cross outside. You aren't cross inside a bit!"

"Indeed! How do you know that?" asked the man.

"Oh, lots of ways. There—like that—the way you act with the dog," she added, pointing to the hand that rested on the dog's head near him. "It's funny how dogs and cats know the insides of folks better than other folks do, isn't it?"

The man did not speak again for some time. Pollyanna wondered if he were asleep. She did not think he was. He looked as if his lips were shut tight to keep back moans of pain.

Minute by minute the time passed. The sun dropped lower in the west and the shadows grew deeper under the trees. Pollyanna sat so still she hardly seemed to breathe. At last the dog pricked up his ears and whined softly. Then he gave a short, sharp bark. The next moment Pollyanna heard voices, and very soon three men appeared carrying a stretcher.

The tallest of the party—a smooth-shaven, kind-eyed man—came forward and asked, "Well, my little lady, playing nurse?"

"Oh, no, sir," smiled Pollyanna. "I haven't given him medicine. But I'm glad I was here."

"So am I," nodded the doctor, as he turned his attention to the injured man.

13. JUST A MATTER OF JELLY

It was about a week after the accident in Pendleton Woods that Pollyanna said to her aunt, "Aunt Polly, please would you mind very much if I took Mrs. Snow's jelly this week to someone else? I'm sure Mrs. Snow wouldn't—this once."

"Dear me, Pollyanna, what are you up to now?" sighed her aunt.

"Nothing, Aunt Polly, truly, that you would mind, I'm sure. You let me take jelly to her, so I thought you would to *him*—this once. You see, broken legs aren't like lifelong invalids, so his won't last forever as Mrs. Snow's does, and she can have all the rest of the things after just once or twice."

"'Him'? 'He'? 'Broken leg'? What are you talking about, Pollyanna?"

"Oh, I forgot you didn't know. I found him in the woods, and I had to unlock his house and telephone for the men and the doctor. And of course then I came away and haven't seen him since. But when Nancy made the jelly for Mrs. Snow this week I thought how nice it would be if I could take it to him instead of her, just this once. Aunt Polly, may I?"

"Yes, yes, I suppose so," agreed Miss Polly, a little wearily. "Who did you say he was?"

"The Man. I mean, Mr. John Pendleton."

Miss Polly almost sprang from her chair. "John Pendleton!"

"Yes. Nancy told me his name. Maybe you know him."

Miss Polly did not answer this. Instead she asked, "Do *you* know him?"

Pollyanna nodded. "Oh, yes. He always speaks and smiles—now. He's only cross outside, you know. I'll go and get the jelly. Nancy had it almost fixed when I came in," finished Pollyanna, already halfway across the room.

"Pollyanna, wait!" Miss Polly's voice was suddenly very stern. "I've changed my mind. I would prefer that Mrs. Snow had that jelly today as usual. That is all. You may go now."

Pollyanna's face fell. "Oh, but Aunt Polly, she can always be sick and have things, but his is just a broken leg. He's had it a whole week now."

"Yes, I remember. I heard Mr. John Pendleton had met with an accident," said Miss Polly, a little stiffly. "But—I do not care to be sending jelly to John Pendleton, Pollyanna."

"I know, he is cross—outside," admitted Pollyanna, sadly, "so I suppose you don't like him. But I wouldn't say it was you sent it. I'd say it was me. I like him. I'd be glad to send him jelly."

Miss Polly began to shake her head again. Then, suddenly, she stopped, and asked in a curiously quiet voice, "Does he know who you are, Pollyanna?"

The little girl sighed. "I reckon not. I told him my name, once, but he never calls me it."

"Does he know where you live?"

"Oh, no. I never told him that."

"Then he doesn't know you're my niece?"

"I don't think so."

For a moment there was silence.

"Very well, Pollyanna," she said at last. "You may take the jelly to Mr. Pendleton as your own gift. But understand, I do not send it. Be very sure that he does not think I do!"

"Yes—no—thank you, Aunt Polly," cried Pollyanna as she flew through the door.

14. Dr. Chilton

The great gray pile of masonry looked very different to Pollyanna when she made her second visit to the house of Mr. John Pendleton. The windows were open, and an elderly woman was hanging out clothes in the back yard. As before, Pollyanna went to the side door. This time she rang the bell. Her fingers were not stiff today from a tight clutch on a bunch of keys.

A familiar-looking small dog bounded up the steps to greet her. There was a slight delay before the woman who had been hanging out clothes opened the door.

"If you please, I've brought some jelly for Mr. Pendleton," smiled Pollyanna.

"Thank you," said the woman, reaching for the bowl. "Who shall I say sent it?"

The doctor, coming into the hall at that moment, heard the woman's words and saw the disappointed look on Pollyanna's face. He stepped quickly forward. "Ah! Some jelly?" he asked genially. "That will be fine! Maybe you'd like to see our patient, eh?"

"Oh, yes, sir," beamed Pollyanna.

The maid led the way through the great library at the end of the hall. Pollyanna saw at once that great changes had taken place. The book-lined walls were the same. But there was no litter on the floor, no untidiness on the desk, and not so much as a grain of dust in sight. One of the mysterious doors was open. The next moment Pollyanna found herself alone with a very cross-looking man lying flat on his back in bed.

"See here, didn't I say—" began an angry voice. "Oh, it's you!"

"Yes, sir," smiled Pollyanna. "Oh, I'm so glad they let me in! You see, at first the lady almost took my jelly, and I was so afraid I wasn't going to see you at all. Then the doctor came, and he said I might. Wasn't he lovely to let me see you?"

In spite of himself, the man's lips twitched into a smile. But all he said was "Humph!"

"And I've brought you some jelly," resumed Pollyanna. "I hope you like it?"

"Never ate it." The fleeting smile had gone, and the scowl had come back to the man's face.

For a brief instant Pollyanna's face showed disappointment. But it cleared as she set the bowl of jelly down. "Didn't you? Well, if you didn't, then you can't know you don't like it, can you? So I reckon I'm glad you haven't, after all. Now, if you knew—"

"Yes, yes. Well, there's one thing I know all right, and that is that I'm flat on my back right here this minute, and that I might have to stay here—till doomsday, I guess."

Pollyanna looked shocked. "Oh, no! Broken legs don't last, you know. So yours won't last till doomsday at all. I should think you could be glad of that."

"Oh, I am," the man said grimly.

"And you didn't break but one. You can be glad it wasn't two."

"Of course! So fortunate," sniffed the man, with uplifted eyebrows. "Looking at it from that standpoint, I suppose I might be glad I wasn't a centipede and didn't break fifty!"

Pollyanna chuckled. "Oh, that's the best yet," she crowed. "I know what a centipede is. They've got lots of legs. Aunt Polly says—"

"Aunt Polly! Well, who is Aunt Polly?"

"She's Miss Polly Harrington. I live with her."

The man made a sudden movement. "Miss—Polly—Harrington!" he breathed.

"Yes. I'm her niece. She's taken me to bring up—on account of my mother, you know," said Pollyanna, in a low voice. "She was her sister. And after father went to be with her and the rest in Heaven, there wasn't anyone left for me down here but the Ladies' Aid. So she took me."

The man did not answer. His face, as he lay back on the pillow, was very white—so white that Pollyanna was frightened. She rose uncertainly to her feet.

"I reckon maybe I'd better go now," she said. "I—I hope you'll like—the jelly."

The man turned his head suddenly, and opened his eyes. There was a curious longing in their dark depths. "And so you are—Miss Polly Harrington's niece," he said gently.

"Yes, sir."

John Pendleton's lips curved in an odd smile. "But—you don't mean—you can't mean that it was Miss Polly Harrington who sent that jelly—to me?" he said slowly.

Pollyanna looked distressed. "N-no, sir: she didn't. She said I must be very sure not to let you think she did send it. But I—"

"I thought as much." The man turned away his head. And Pollyanna, still more distressed, tiptoed from the room.

Outside she found the doctor waiting in his gig.

"Well, Miss Pollyanna, may I have the pleasure of seeing you home?" asked the doctor with a smile. "I started to drive on a few minutes ago, but then I thought I'd wait for you."

"Thank you, sir. I'm glad you did. I just love to ride," beamed Pollyanna.

"Do you?" smiled the doctor. "Well, as near as I can judge, there are a good many things you 'love' to do—eh?" he added, as they drove briskly away.

Pollyanna laughed. "Why, I don't know. I reckon perhaps there are," she admitted. "I like to do 'most everything." Then she added, "Dr. Chilton, I should think being a doctor would be the very gladdest kind of a business there was."

"'Gladdest'! When I see so much suffering always, everywhere I go?" he cried.

She nodded. "I know. But you're *helping* it—don't you see? And of course you're glad to help it! And so that makes you the gladdest of any of us, all the time."

The doctor looked into Pollyanna's shining eyes. He felt as if a loving hand had been laid on his head in blessing. His life was a lonely one. He had no wife, and his work was dear to him. He gave Pollyanna a bright smile, which his patients knew and loved so well. The doctor left Pollyanna at her own door, smiled at Nancy, who was sweeping off the front porch, then drove rapidly away.

Pollyanna found her aunt in the sitting room.

"Who was that man—the one who drove into the yard, Pollyanna?" questioned the lady a little sharply.

"Why, Aunt Polly, that was Dr. Chilton! Don't you know him?"

"Dr. Chilton! What was he doing here?"

"He drove me home. Oh, and I gave the jelly to Mr. Pendleton, and—"

Miss Polly lifted her head quickly. "Pollyanna, he did not think I sent it?"

"Oh, no, Aunt Polly. I told him you didn't."

Miss Polly grew a vivid pink. "You *told* him I didn't!"

Pollyanna opened her eyes wide. "Why, Aunt Polly, you said to!"

"I said, Pollyanna, that I did not send it, and for you to be very sure that he did not think I did! Which is a very different matter from telling him that I did not send it."

"Well, I don't see where the difference is," sighed Pollyanna, as she went to hang her hat on the one hook in the house upon which Aunt Polly had said that it must be hung.

15. A RED ROSE AND A LACE SHAWL

It was a rainy day, about a week after Pollyanna's visit to Mr. John Pendleton. Miss Polly was driven by Timothy to a meeting. When she returned, her cheeks were a bright, pretty pink, and her hair, blown by the damp wind, had fluffed into curls wherever the loosened pins had given leave.

Pollyanna had never before seen her aunt look like this.

"Why, Aunt Polly, you've got 'em, too," she cried as that lady entered the sitting room.

"Got what, you impossible child?"

Pollyanna danced round her aunt. "And I never knew you had 'em! Can folks have 'em when you don't know they've got 'em? Do you suppose I could?" she cried, pulling out with eager fingers the straight locks above her ears.

"Pollyanna, what does all this mean?" demanded Aunt Polly, removing her hat and trying to smooth back her disordered hair.

"No, no—please, Aunt Polly!" Pollyanna cried. "Don't smooth 'em out! It's those that I'm talking about—those little black curls. Oh, Aunt Polly, they're so pretty!"

"Nonsense!"

"But it isn't nonsense," urged Pollyanna. "You don't know how pretty you look with your hair like that! Oh, Aunt Polly, please, may I do your hair like I did Mrs. Snow's, and put in a flower? I'd so love to see you that way! Why, you'd be ever so much prettier than she was!"

"Pollyanna!" Miss Polly spoke very sharply—all the more sharply because Pollyanna's words had given her an odd throb of joy. When before had anybody cared how she or her hair looked? When before had anybody loved to see her pretty?

"Now wait just where you are. I'll get a comb."

"But Pollyanna," protested Aunt Polly, following the little girl upstairs.

Pollyanna greeted her at the door of Miss Polly's own room. "I've got the comb. Now sit down, please, right here. Oh, I'm so glad you let me do it!"

"But, Pollyanna, I—"

In helpless amazement, Miss Polly found herself in the chair before the dressing table, with her hair already tumbling about her ears under ten eager but very gentle fingers.

"Oh, my! What pretty hair you've got," chattered Pollyanna. " Why, Aunt Polly, I'll make you so pretty everybody'll just love to look at you!"

"Pollyanna!" gasped a shocked voice from a veil of hair. "I—I'm sure I don't know why I'm letting you do this silly thing."

"Oh, Aunt Polly, I've just happened to think of something! But it's a secret, and I can't tell. Now your hair is almost done, and I'm going to leave you just a minute. And you must promise—*promise*—not to stir nor peek till I come back. Now remember!" she finished, as she ran from the room.

Aloud Miss Polly said nothing. To herself she said that of course she should at once undo her niece's absurd work and put her hair up properly again.

At that moment, Miss Polly caught a glimpse of herself in the mirror of the dressing table. And what she saw sent such a flush of color to her cheeks that she only flushed more at the sight.

She saw a face—not young, it is true—but just now bright with excitement and surprise. The cheeks were a pretty pink. The eyes sparkled. The hair, dark, and still damp from the outdoor air, lay in loose waves about the forehead and curved back over the ears in wonderfully becoming lines, with softening little curls here and there.

So amazed was Miss Polly with what she saw in the glass that she quite forgot her determination to do over her hair, until she heard Pollyanna enter the room again. Before she could move, then, she felt a folded something slipped across her eyes and tied in the back.

"Pollyanna, Pollyanna! What are you doing?" she cried.

Pollyanna chuckled. "That's just what I don't want you to know, Aunt Polly, and I was afraid you would peek, so I tied on the handkerchief. Now sit still. It won't take but just a minute, then I'll let you see."

"But, Pollyanna," began Miss Polly, struggling blindly to her feet, "you must take this off! You—child, child! What are you doing?" she gasped, as she felt a soft something slipped about her shoulders. Pollyanna only chuckled. She was draping about her aunt's shoulders the fleecy folds of a beautiful lace shawl, yellowed from long years of packing away, and fragrant with lavender. Pollyanna had found the shawl in the attic the week before.

Her task completed, Pollyanna pulled her aunt toward the sun parlor, where a red rose bloomed on the trellis.

"Pollyanna, where are you taking me?" Aunt Polly vainly tried to hold herself back. "Pollyanna, I shall not—"

"It's just to the sun parlor!" panted Pollyanna, reaching for the rose and thrusting it into the soft hair above Miss Polly's ear. "There!" She untied the knot of the handkerchief. "Oh, Aunt Polly, now you'll be glad I dressed you up!"

For one dazed moment Miss Polly looked at herself, and at her surroundings. Then she gave a low cry and fled to her room. Pollyanna, following the direction of her aunt's last dismayed gaze, saw through the window a horse and gig turning into the driveway. She recognized the man who held the reins.

"Dr. Chilton, Dr. Chilton! Did you want to see me? I'm up here."

"Yes," smiled the doctor, a little gravely. "Will you come down, please?"

In the bedroom Pollyanna found a flushed-faced, angry-eyed woman plucking at the pins that held a lace shawl in place. "Pollyanna, how could you?" moaned the woman. "To think of your rigging me up like this, and then letting me be seen!"

Pollyanna stopped in dismay. "But you looked lovely—perfectly lovely, Aunt Polly, and—"

"'Lovely'!" scorned the woman, flinging the shawl to one side and attacking her hair with shaking fingers.

"Oh, Aunt Polly, please, please let the hair stay!"

"Stay? Like this? As if I would!" And Miss Polly pulled the locks so tightly back that the last curl lay stretched dead at the ends of her fingers.

"And you did look so pretty," sobbed Pollyanna, as she stumbled through the door.

Downstairs Pollyanna found the doctor waiting in his gig.

"I've prescribed you for a patient, and he's sent me to get the prescription filled," announced the doctor. "It's Mr. John Pendleton. He would like to see you today, if you'll be so good as to come. Will you come? I'll bring you back before six o'clock."

"I'd love to!" exclaimed Pollyanna. "Let me ask Aunt Polly."

In a few moments she returned, hat in hand, but with rather a sober face.

"Didn't your aunt want you to go?" asked the doctor as they drove away.

"Yes," sighed Pollyanna. "She—she wanted me to go too much, I'm afraid."

"Wanted you to go too much!"

Pollyanna sighed again. "Yes. I reckon she meant she didn't want me there. You see, she said: 'Yes, yes, run along, run along—do! I wish you'd gone before.'"

The doctor smiled, but his eyes were grave. Then he asked, "Wasn't it your aunt I saw with you a few minutes ago, in the window of the sun parlor?"

Pollyanna drew a long breath. "Yes, that's what's the whole trouble, I suppose. You see I'd dressed her up in a perfectly lovely lace shawl I found upstairs, and I'd fixed her hair and put on a rose, and she looked so pretty. Didn't you think she looked just lovely?"

For a moment the doctor did not answer. When he did speak his voice was so low Pollyanna could but just hear the words. "Yes, Pollyanna, I—I thought she did look just lovely."

"Did you? I'm so glad! I'll tell her," nodded the little girl, contentedly.

To her surprise the doctor gave a sudden exclamation. "Never! Pollyanna, I—I'm afraid I shall have to ask you not to tell her—that."

"Why, Dr. Chilton! Why not? I should think you'd be glad—"

"But she might not be," cut in the doctor.

Pollyanna considered this for a moment. "That's so—maybe she wouldn't," she sighed. "I remember now. It was 'cause she saw you that she ran."

The doctor said nothing. He did not speak again, indeed, until they were almost to the great stone house in which John Pendleton lay with a broken leg.

16. "Just Like a Book"

John Pendleton greeted Pollyanna with a smile. "Well, Miss Pollyanna, you must be a very forgiving little person, or you wouldn't have come to see me again today."

"Why, Mr. Pendleton, I was glad to come, and I'm sure I don't see why I shouldn't be."

"Oh, well, I was pretty cross with you, I'm afraid, both the other day when you so kindly brought me the jelly, and that time when you found me with the broken leg at first. By the way, I don't think I've ever thanked you for that."

"But I was glad to find you—that is, I don't mean I was glad your leg was broken, of course," she corrected hurriedly.

John Pendleton smiled. "I understand. I do thank you, and I consider you a very brave little girl to do what you did that day. I thank you for the jelly, too," he added.

"Did you like it?" asked Pollyanna with interest.

"Very much. I suppose there isn't any more today that—that Aunt Polly *didn't* send, is there?" he asked with an odd smile.

"N-no, sir." She hesitated, then went on with a blush. "Please, Mr. Pendleton, I didn't mean to be rude the other day when I said Aunt Polly did *not* send the jelly."

There was no answer. John Pendleton was not smiling now. After a time he drew a long sigh and turned to Pollyanna. "Well, well, this will never do at all! I didn't send for you to see me moping this time. Listen! Out in the library—the big room where the telephone is, you know—you will find a carved box on the lower shelf of the big case with glass doors in the corner not far from the fireplace. You may bring it to me. It is heavy, but not too heavy for you to carry, I think."

"Oh, I'm awfully strong," declared Pollyanna as she sprang to her feet. In a minute she had returned with the box.

It was a wonderful half-hour that Pollyanna spent then. The box was full of treasures that John Pendleton had picked up in years of travel. For each there was some entertaining story, whether it were a set of finely carved chessmen from China, or a little jade statue from India.

The visit was delightful, but before it was over, Pollyanna realized that they were talking about something besides the wonderful things in the beautiful carved box. They were talking of herself, of Nancy, of Aunt Polly, and of her daily life. They were talking, too, even of the life and home long ago in the far Western town.

Not until it was nearly time for her to go did the man say, in a voice Pollyanna had never before heard from stern John Pendleton, "I thought, at first, after I found out who you were, that I didn't want you to come anymore. You reminded me of—of something I have tried for long years to forget. So I said to myself that I never wanted to see you again. But after a time I found I wanted to see you so much that not seeing you was making me remember even more the thing I was trying to forget. So now I want you to come. Will you?"

"Why, yes, Mr. Pendleton," breathed Pollyanna, her eyes glowing with sympathy for the sad-faced man lying back on the pillow before her. "I'd love to come!"

"Thank you," said John Pendleton, gently.

After supper that evening, Pollyanna sat on the back porch and told Nancy all about Mr. John Pendleton's wonderful carved box, and the still more wonderful things it contained.

"And to think," sighed Nancy, "that he showed you all them things, and told you about 'em like that—him that's so cross he never talks to no one—no one!"

"Oh, but he isn't cross, Nancy, only outside," Pollyanna observed, with quick loyalty. "I don't see why everybody thinks he's so bad, either. They wouldn't, if they knew him. But even Aunt Polly doesn't like him very well. She wouldn't send the jelly to him, you know, and she was so afraid he'd think she did send it!"

"But what beats me," said Nancy, "is how he happened to take to you so, Miss Pollyanna. He ain't the sort of man what generally takes to kids."

Pollyanna smiled. "Why, only today he said that one time he felt he never wanted to see me again, because I reminded him of something he wanted to forget. But afterwards—"

"What's that?" interrupted Nancy. "He said you reminded him of something he wanted to forget?"

"Yes. But afterwards—"

"What was it?" Nancy asked eagerly.

"He didn't tell me. He just said it was something."

"Oh, Miss Pollyanna! It's a *mystery!* Why, that's just like a book—I've read lots of 'em. All of 'em had mysteries and things just like this. My stars and stockings! Just think of havin' a book lived right under your nose like this! No wonder he took to you. No wonder!"

"But he didn't," cried Pollyanna, "not till I talked to him, first. And he didn't even know who I was till I took the jelly, and had to make him understand that Aunt Polly didn't send it, and—"

Nancy sprang to her feet. "Oh, Miss Pollyanna, I know— I KNOW!" The next minute she was down at Pollyanna's side again. "Tell me—now think," she urged. "It was after he found out you was Miss Polly's niece that he said he didn't ever want to see you again, wasn't it?"

"Oh, yes. I told him that the last time I saw him, and he told me this today."

"I thought as much," crowed Nancy. "And Miss Polly wouldn't send the jelly herself, would she?"

"No."

"And you told him she didn't send it?"

"Why, yes, I—"

"And he began to act strange after he found out you was her niece. Didn't he?"

"Why, yes, he did act a little strange over that jelly," admitted Pollyanna.

Nancy drew a long sigh. "Then I've got it, sure! Now listen. *Mr. John Pendleton was in love with Miss Polly Harrington!*" she announced.

"Why, Nancy, he couldn't be! She doesn't like him," objected Pollyanna.

"Of course she don't! That's the quarrel!" Nancy happily settled herself to tell the story. "Just before you come, Mr. Tom told me Miss Polly had been in love once. I couldn't believe it—her! But Mr. Tom said she had, and that the man was livin' now right in this town. And now I know it's John Pendleton. Hasn't he got a mystery in his life? Don't he shut himself up in that grand house alone, and never speak to no one? Didn't he act strange when he found out you was Miss Polly's niece? And now hasn't he said that you remind him of somethin' he wants to forget? Why, Miss Pollyanna, it's as plain as the nose on your face."

"Oh!" breathed Pollyanna, in wide-eyed amazement. "But, Nancy, I should think if they loved each other they'd make up sometime. Both of 'em all alone, all these years!"

Nancy sniffed. "I guess maybe you don't know much about lovers' quarrels, Miss Pollyanna. You ain't big enough yet, anyhow."

Pollyanna said nothing. But her face was very thoughtful. She never doubted now that John Pendleton and Aunt Polly had once been in love. And, with all her heart, she wished she could in some way bring happiness into their lonely lives.

But she could not see just how she was to do this. She talked to Mr. Pendleton about her aunt. He listened, sometimes politely, sometimes irritably, often with a puzzled smile. She talked to her aunt about Mr. Pendleton. But Miss Polly would not listen long. She always found something else to talk about. But she often did that whenever Pollyanna talked of others—of Dr. Chilton, for instance. Aunt Polly, indeed, seemed very bitter against Dr. Chilton, as Pollyanna found out one day when a cold shut her up in the house.

"If you are not better by night I shall send for the doctor," Aunt Polly said.

"Shall you? Then I'm going to be worse," said Pollyanna. "I'd love to have Dr. Chilton come to see me!"

"It will not be Dr. Chilton, Pollyanna," Miss Polly said sternly. "Dr. Chilton is not our family physician. I shall send for Dr. Warren—if you are worse."

Pollyanna did not grow worse, however, and Dr. Warren was not summoned.

"And I'm so glad, too," Pollyanna said to her aunt that evening. "Of course I like Dr. Warren, but I like Dr. Chilton better, and I'm afraid he'd feel hurt if I didn't have him."

"That will do, Pollyanna. I really do not wish to discuss Dr. Chilton—or his feelings."

Pollyanna looked at her for a moment. Then she sighed, "I just love to see you when your cheeks are pink like that, Aunt Polly. But I would so like to fix your hair. If—"

But her aunt was already out of sight down the hall.

17. Which Is Somewhat Surprising

Pollyanna entered school in September. She was soon a happy member of a class of girls and boys her own age. School, in some ways, was a surprise to Pollyanna. And Pollyanna, in many ways, was very much of a surprise to school. They were soon on the best of terms, however.

In spite of her delight in her new work, Pollyanna did not forget her old friends. True, she could not give them quite so much time now, but she gave them what time she could. Of them all, perhaps John Pendleton was the most dissatisfied.

One Saturday afternoon he spoke to her about it. "See here, Pollyanna, how would you like to come and live with me?" he asked, a little impatiently. "I don't see anything of you, nowadays."

Pollyanna laughed. "I thought you didn't like to have folks 'round," she said.

He made a wry face. "Oh, but that was before you taught me to play that game of yours."

"Oh, but you aren't really glad at all for things. You just say you are," said Pollyanna. "You know you don't play the game right *ever*, Mr. Pendleton!"

The man's face grew suddenly very grave. "That's why I want you—to help me play it. Will you come?"

Pollyanna looked distressed. "Why, Mr. Pendleton, I can't. You know I can't. Why, I'm Aunt Polly's!"

A look crossed the man's face that Pollyanna could not quite understand. His head came up almost fiercely. "You're no more hers than—Perhaps she would let you come to me," he finished more gently. "Would you come—if she did?"

Pollyanna frowned in deep thought. "But Aunt Polly has been so—good to me," she began. "And she took me when I didn't have anybody left but the Ladies' Aid, and—"

This time, when he spoke, his voice was low and very sad. "Pollyanna, long years ago I loved somebody very much. I hoped to bring her, someday, to this house. I pictured how happy we'd be together in our home all the long years to come."

"Yes," pitied Pollyanna, her eyes shining with sympathy.

"But—well, I didn't bring her here. Never mind why. And ever since then this great gray pile of stone has been a house—never a home. It takes a woman's hand and heart, or a child's presence, to make a home, Pollyanna, and I have not had either. Now will you come, my dear?"

Pollyanna sprang to her feet. Her face lit up. "Mr. Pendleton, you—you mean that you wish you had had that woman's hand and heart all this time?"

"Why, yes, Pollyanna."

"Oh, I'm so glad! Then it's all right," sighed the little girl. "Now you can take us both, and everything will be lovely."

"Take you *both?*" repeated the man.

A faint doubt crossed Pollyanna's face. "Well, of course, Aunt Polly isn't won over, yet. But I'm sure she will be if you tell it to her just as you did to me, and then we'd both come, of course."

A look of actual terror leaped to the man's eyes. "Aunt Polly come *here!*"

Pollyanna's eyes widened a little. "Would you rather go there?" she asked. "Of course the house isn't quite so pretty, but it's nearer—"

"Pollyanna, what are you talking about?" asked the man, very gently now.

"Why, about where we're going to live," replied Pollyanna with surprise. "You said it was here that you had wanted Aunt Polly's hand and heart all these years to make a home, and—"

A cry came from the man's throat. He raised his hand and began to speak. But the next moment he dropped his hand at his side.

"The doctor, sir," said the maid in the doorway.

Pollyanna rose at once. John Pendleton turned to her feverishly. "Pollyanna, for Heaven's sake, say nothing of what I asked you—yet," he begged, in a low voice.

Pollyanna gave a sunny smile. "Of course not! Just as if I didn't know you'd rather tell her yourself!"

John Pendleton fell limply back in his chair.

"Why, what's up?" demanded the doctor, a minute later, his fingers on his patient's galloping pulse.

A smile trembled on John Pendleton's lips. "Overdose of your—prescription, I guess," he laughed, as he noted the doctor's eyes following Pollyanna's little figure down the driveway.

18. WHICH IS MORE SURPRISING

Sunday mornings Pollyanna usually attended church and Sunday school. Sunday afternoons she frequently went for a walk with Nancy. She had planned one for the day after her Saturday afternoon visit to Mr. John Pendleton. But on the way home from Sunday school Dr. Chilton overtook her in his gig and brought his horse to a stop.

"Suppose you let me drive you home, Pollyanna," he suggested. "I was just driving out to your place to tell you," he went on, as Pollyanna settled herself at his side. "Mr.

Pendleton sent a special request for you to go to see him this afternoon. He says it's very important."

Pollyanna nodded happily. "Yes, it is, I know. I'll go."

The doctor eyed her with some surprise. "I'm not sure I shall let you, after all," he declared, his eyes twinkling. "You seemed more upsetting than soothing yesterday, young lady."

Pollyanna laughed. "Oh, it wasn't me—not really. Not so much as it was Aunt Polly."

The doctor turned with a quick start. "Your—aunt!" he exclaimed.

Pollyanna gave a happy little bounce in her seat. "Yes. And it's so exciting and lovely, just like a story, you know. I—I'm going to tell you," she burst out, with sudden decision. "He said not to mention it. But he wouldn't mind your knowing, of course. He meant not to mention it to *her.*"

"Her?"

"Yes. Aunt Polly. And, of course he would want to tell her himself—about being in love!"

"In *love!*" As the doctor said the word, the horse started violently, as if the hand that held the reins had given them a sharp jerk.

"Yes," nodded Pollyanna, happily. "That's the story-part, you see. I didn't know it till Nancy told me. She said Aunt Polly had a love affair years ago, but there was a quarrel. She didn't know who it was at first. But we've found out now. It's Mr. Pendleton, you know."

The doctor relaxed suddenly. "Oh! No. I—didn't know," he said quietly.

"Yes, and I'm so glad now. It's come out lovely. Mr. Pendleton asked me to come and live with him, but of course I wouldn't leave Aunt Polly like that—after she'd been so good to me. Then he told me all about the woman's hand and heart that he used to want, and I found out that he wanted it now. And I was so glad! For of course if he wants to make up the quarrel, everything will be all right now, and Aunt Polly and I will both go to live there, or else he'll come to live with us. Of course Aunt Polly doesn't know yet, and we haven't got everything settled. So I suppose that is why he wanted to see me this afternoon."

There was an odd smile on the doctor's lips. "Yes. I can well imagine that Mr. John Pendleton does want to see you, Pollyanna." He pulled his horse to a stop before the door.

"There's Aunt Polly now in the window," cried Pollyanna. Then, a second later: "Why, no, she isn't—but I thought I saw her!"

"No, she isn't there—now," said the doctor. His lips had suddenly lost their smile.

Pollyanna found a very nervous John Pendleton waiting for her that afternoon. "Pollyanna," he began at once. "I've been trying all night to puzzle out what you meant by all that, yesterday—about my wanting your Aunt Polly's hand and heart here all those years. What did you mean?"

"Why, because you were in love once. And I was so glad you still felt that way now."

"In love! Your Aunt Polly and I?"

At the obvious surprise in the man's voice, Pollyanna opened wide her eyes. "Why, Mr. Pendleton, Nancy said you were!"

The man gave a short little laugh. "Indeed! Well, I'm afraid that Nancy didn't know."

"Then you weren't?" Pollyanna's voice was tragic with dismay.

"Never!"

"And it *isn't* all coming out like a book?"

There was no answer. The man's eyes were fixed out the window.

"Oh dear! And it was all going so splendidly," almost sobbed Pollyanna. "I'd have been so glad to come—with Aunt Polly."

"And you won't—now?" The man asked the question without turning his head.

"Of course not! I'm Aunt Polly's."

The man turned now, almost fiercely. "Before you were hers, Pollyanna, you were your mother's. And it was your mother's hand and heart that I wanted long years ago."

"My mother's!"

"Yes. I had not meant to tell you, but perhaps it's better, after all, that I do." John Pendleton's face had grown very white. "I loved your mother, but she didn't love me. And after a time she went away with your father. The whole world suddenly seemed to turn black under my fingers, and—but never mind. For long years I have been a cross, crabbed, unlovable, unloved old man. Then, one day, you danced into my life. And now I want you always."

"But, Mr. Pendleton, what about Aunt Polly?" Pollyanna's eyes were blurred with tears.

The man made an impatient gesture. "What about me? How do you suppose I'm going to be 'glad' about anything—without you? Why, Pollyanna, it's only since you came that I've been even half glad to live! But if I had you for my own little girl, I'd be glad for anything, and I'd try to make you glad, too, my dear."

"Aunt Polly has been so good to me," she began. But the man interrupted her sharply.

"Of course she's been good to you! But she doesn't want you half so much as I do."

"Why, Mr. Pendleton, she's glad, I know, to have—"

"Glad!" interrupted the man, losing his patience now. "I'll wager Miss Polly doesn't know how to be glad—for anything! Everyone knows her, and she isn't the 'glad' kind, Pollyanna. As for your coming to me—you just ask her and see if she won't let you come."

Pollyanna rose to her feet with a long sigh. "All right. I'll ask her," she said. "Of course I don't mean that I wouldn't like to live here with you, Mr. Pendleton, but—" There was a moment's silence, then she added: "Anyhow, I'm glad I didn't tell her yesterday. 'Cause then I supposed she was wanted, too."

John Pendleton smiled grimly. "Well, yes, Pollyanna. I guess it is just as well you didn't mention it yesterday."

"I didn't—only to the doctor, and of course he doesn't count."

"The doctor!" cried John Pendleton, turning quickly. "Not Dr. Chilton?"

"Yes, when he came to tell me you wanted to see me today, you know."

"Well, of all the—" muttered the man. "And what did Dr. Chilton say?"

Pollyanna frowned thoughtfully. "Why, I don't remember. Not much—just that he could well imagine you did want to see me."

"Oh, did he, indeed!" answered John Pendleton, with a strange little laugh.

19. A QUESTION ANSWERED

The sky was darkening fast with an approaching thunder-shower when Pollyanna hurried down the hill from John Pendleton's house. Halfway home she met Nancy with an umbrella.

"Miss Polly wanted me to come with this. She was *worried* about you!"

"Oh," sighed Pollyanna. "I'm sorry. I didn't mean to scare her."

"Well, I'm glad," replied Nancy, unexpectedly. "I am, I am."

Pollyanna stared. "Glad that Aunt Polly was scared about me! Why, Nancy, that isn't the way to play the game—to be glad for things like that!" she objected.

"There wasn't no game in it," replied Nancy. "You don't seem to sense what it means to have Miss Polly worried about you, child!"

"Why, it means worried—and worried is horrid to feel. What else can it mean?"

Nancy tossed her head. "Well, I'll tell you what it means. It means she's at last gettin' down somewhere near human—like folks. And that she ain't just doin' her duty by you all the time."

Pollyanna's brows drew into a troubled frown. "Nancy," she sighed, "do you think Aunt Polly likes to have me here? Would she mind if I wasn't here anymore?"

"Likes to have you here? Would she miss you if you wasn't here?" cried Nancy. "As if that wasn't just what I was tellin' you! Didn't she send me with an umbrella 'cause she saw a little cloud in the sky? Didn't she make me tote your things all downstairs, so you could have the pretty room you

wanted? Why, Miss Pollyanna, when you remember how at first she hated to have—" With a choking cough Nancy paused just in time.

"Oh, Nancy, I'm so glad! You don't know how glad I am that Aunt Polly wants *me!*"

Later, as she climbed the stairs to her room, she thought, "I always knew I wanted to live with Aunt Polly. But maybe I didn't know quite how much I wanted Aunt Polly—to want to live with *me?*"

It would not be easy to tell John Pendleton of her decision, and Pollyanna dreaded the task. She was very fond of John Pendleton. And she was very sorry for him, because he seemed to be so sorry for himself. She was sorry, too, for the long, lonely life that had made him so unhappy. And she was grieved that it had been because of her mother that he had spent those dreary years. She wished that somewhere, someone might be found who—and at this point she sprang to her feet with a little cry of joy at the thought that had come to her.

As soon as she could, she hurried up the hill to John Pendleton's house. Soon she found herself in the great dim library, with John Pendleton himself sitting near her. His long, thin hands lay idle on the arms of his chair, and his faithful little dog sat at his feet.

"Well, Pollyanna, is it to be the 'glad game' with me, all the rest of my life?" asked the man.

"Oh, yes," cried Pollyanna. "I've thought of the very gladdest thing for you to do, and—"

"With you?" asked John Pendleton, his mouth growing a little stern at the corners.

"N-no, but—"

"Pollyanna, you aren't going to say no!"

"I—I've got to, Mr. Pendleton, truly I have. Aunt Polly—"

"Did she refuse to let you come?"

"I—I didn't ask her," stammered the little girl, miserably.

"Pollyanna!"

Pollyanna turned away her eyes. She could not meet the hurt gaze of her friend.

"So you didn't even ask her!"

"I couldn't, sir—truly," faltered Pollyanna. "You see, I found out without asking. Aunt Polly wants me with her, and—and I want to stay, too," she confessed bravely. "You don't know how good she's been to me. And I think, really, sometimes she's beginning to be glad about things. And you know she never used to be. Oh, Mr. Pendleton, I couldn't leave Aunt Polly now!"

There was a long pause. Only the snapping of the wood fire broke the silence. At last, however, the man spoke. "No, Pollyanna. I see," he said. "I won't ask you again."

"Oh, but you don't know about the rest of it," she reminded him eagerly. "There's the very gladdest thing you *can* do—truly there is!"

"Not for me, Pollyanna."

"Yes, sir, for you. You said it. You said only a woman's hand and heart or a child's presence could make a home. And I can get it for you—a child's presence—not me, you know, but another one."

"Another! Who?"

"Jimmy Bean. He's the 'child's presence,' you know, and he'll be so glad to be it!"

"Will he? Well, I won't," exclaimed the man. "Pollyanna, this is sheer nonsense!"

"You don't mean—you won't take him?"

"I certainly do mean just that."

"But he'd be a lovely child's presence," faltered Pollyanna. She was almost crying now. "And you couldn't be lonesome with Jimmy around."

"I don't doubt it," replied the man, "but—I think I prefer the lonesomeness."

It was then that Pollyanna remembered something Nancy had once told her. She raised her chin. "Maybe you think a nice live little boy wouldn't be better than that old dead skeleton you keep, but I think it would!"

"*Skeleton?*"

"Yes. Nancy said you had one in your closet, somewhere."

"Why, what—" Suddenly the man threw back his head and laughed. "Pollyanna, I suspect you are right—more right than you know," he said gently.

20. An Accident

At Mrs. Snow's request, Pollyanna went one day to Dr. Chilton's office to get the name of a medicine that Mrs. Snow had forgotten. "I've never been to your home before! This is your home, isn't it?" she said, looking interestedly about her.

The doctor smiled a little sadly. "Yes—such as it is," he answered, as he wrote something on a pad of paper. "But it's a pretty poor excuse for a home, Pollyanna. They're just rooms, that's all—not a home."

Pollyanna nodded her head wisely. Her eyes glowed with sympathetic understanding.

"I know. It takes a woman's hand and heart, or a child's presence to make a home," she said.

"Eh?" The doctor wheeled about.

"Mr. Pendleton told me," nodded Pollyanna. "Why don't you get a woman's hand and heart, Dr. Chilton? Or maybe you'd take Jimmy Bean—if Mr. Pendleton doesn't want him."

Dr. Chilton laughed a little. "So Mr. Pendleton says it takes a woman's hand and heart to make a home, does he?" he asked.

"Yes. He says his is just a house, too. Why don't you, Dr. Chilton?"

"Why don't I what?" The doctor had turned back to his desk.

"Get a woman's hand and heart. Oh—and I forgot." Pollyanna suddenly blushed. "I suppose I ought to tell you. It wasn't Aunt Polly that Mr. Pendleton loved long ago. And so we aren't going there to live. I made a mistake. I hope you didn't tell any one," she finished anxiously.

"No—I didn't tell anyone, Pollyanna," replied the doctor, a little strangely.

"Oh, that's all right, then," sighed Pollyanna in relief. But why don't you get a woman's hand and heart, Dr. Chilton?"

There was a moment's silence. Then very gravely the doctor said, "They're not always to be had for the asking, little girl."

Pollyanna frowned. Then her eyes widened in surprise. "Why, Dr. Chilton. You didn't try to get somebody's hand and heart once, like Mr. Pendleton, and—and couldn't?"

The doctor got to his feet. "There, there, Pollyanna, never mind about that. Don't let other people's troubles worry your little head. Suppose you run back now to Mrs. Snow. I've written down the name of the medicine. Was there anything else?"

Pollyanna shook her head. "No, sir. Thank you, sir," she murmured thoughtfully as she turned toward the door.

It was on the last day of October that the accident occurred. Pollyanna, hurrying home from school, crossed the road at an apparently safe distance in front of a swiftly approaching motor car.

Just what happened, no one could seem to tell afterward. Neither was there anyone found who could tell why it happened or who was to blame that it did happen. Pollyanna, however, at five o'clock, was carried, limp and unconscious, into the little room that was so dear to her. There, a white-faced Aunt Polly and a weeping Nancy undressed her tenderly and put her to bed. From the village, Dr. Warren hurried as fast as another motor car could bring him.

There appeared to be no bones broken, but the doctor had looked very grave, had shaken his head slowly, and had said that time alone could tell. After he had gone, Miss Polly's face was pale and strained. The patient had not fully recovered consciousness, but she seemed to be resting as comfortably as could be expected. A trained nurse had been sent for, and would come that night. That was all. And Nancy turned, sobbing, and went back to her kitchen.

It was late the next morning that Pollyanna opened her eyes and realized where she was. "Why, Aunt Polly, what's the matter? Isn't it daytime? Why don't I get up?" she cried. "Why, Aunt Polly, I can't get up," she moaned, falling back on the pillow.

"No, dear, I wouldn't try—just yet," soothed her aunt quickly, but very quietly.

"But what is the matter? Why can't I get up?"

Miss Polly tried to swallow the lump that would scarcely let her speak. "You were hurt, dear, by the automobile last night. But never mind that now. Auntie wants you to rest again."

"Hurt? Oh, yes, I—I ran." Pollyanna's eyes were dazed. She lifted her hand to her forehead. "Why, it—hurts!"

"Yes, dear, but never mind. Just—just rest."

"But, Aunt Polly, I feel so funny, and so bad! My legs feel so—so strange—only they don't FEEL at all!"

After a week had passed, the fever passed, the pain lessened, and Pollyanna's mind was clear again. She then had to be told all over again what had occurred.

"And so I'm hurt, and not sick," she sighed at last. "Well, I'm glad of that."

"Glad, Pollyanna?" asked her aunt, who was sitting by the bed.

"Yes. I'd so much rather have broken legs like Mr. Pendleton's than lifelong invalids like Mrs. Snow, you know. Broken legs get well, and lifelong invalids don't."

Miss Polly—who had said nothing whatever about broken legs—got suddenly to her feet and walked to the little dressing table across the room.

"I'm glad it isn't smallpox, too," Pollyanna murmured. "That would be worse than freckles. And I'm glad it isn't whooping cough—I've had that, and it's horrid. And I'm glad it isn't measles, 'cause they're catching, and they wouldn't let you stay here."

"You seem to—to be glad for a good many things, my dear," Aunt Polly said quietly.

Pollyanna laughed softly. "I am. I'm glad of things I haven't said. I'm almost glad I was hurt."

"Pollyanna!"

Pollyanna turned shining eyes on her aunt. "Well, you see, since I have been hurt, you've called me 'dear' lots of times—and you didn't before. I love to be called 'dear.' Some of the Ladies' Aiders did call me that, and of course that was pretty nice, but not so nice as if they had belonged to me, like you do. Oh, Aunt Polly, I'm so glad you belong to me!"

Aunt Polly did not answer. Her eyes were full of tears.

It was that afternoon that Nancy ran out to Old Tom in the barn. "Mr. Tom, Mr. Tom. Guess what's happened," she panted. "You couldn't guess in a thousand years—you couldn't, you couldn't!"

"Then I won't try," replied the man. "You'd better tell me first off, Nancy."

"Well, listen, then. Who do you suppose is in the parlor now with the mistress? Who?"

Old Tom shook his head. "There's no tellin'," he declared.

"Yes, there is. I'm tellin'. It's John Pendleton! Just think, Mr. Tom—HIM callin' on HER!"

"Well, why not?" demanded the old man.

"Well, I've been askin' folks about him some," said Nancy. "I heard somethin' that made me think him an' Miss Polly was in love."

"MR. PENDLETON!" Old Tom straightened up.

"Oh, I know now, it wasn't Miss Polly. It was that blessed child's mother he was in love with. Well, now I've found out that him an' Miss Polly haven't been friends for years, and that she's been hatin' him like poison 'cause of the silly gossip that coupled their names together when she was eighteen or twenty."

"Yes, I remember," nodded Old Tom. "It was three or four years after Miss Jennie went off with the other chap. Miss Polly knew about it, of course, and was sorry for him. So she tried to be nice to him. Maybe she overdid it a little. Anyway, somebody begun to make trouble. They said she was runnin' after him."

"Runnin' after any man—her!" exclaimed Nancy.

"I know it. But that's what they said," declared Old Tom, "and of course no gal can stand that. Then come that other feller and the trouble with *him.* After that she shut up like an oyster and wouldn't have nothin' to do with nobody. Her heart just seemed to turn bitter at the core."

"Yes, I've heard about that now," replied Nancy. "And that's why you could have knocked me down with a feather when I saw him at the door—him, what she hasn't spoke to for years!"

"Humph!" grunted Old Tom, and fell to work again.

In the parlor, Mr. John Pendleton did not have to wait long before a swift step warned him of Miss Polly's coming. Her face was cold.

"I called to ask about Pollyanna," he began at once.

"Thank you. She is about the same," said Miss Polly.

"And—won't you tell me how she is?" His voice was not quite steady this time.

Pain crossed the woman's face. "I can't. I wish I could!"

"You mean you don't know? But the doctor?"

"Dr. Warren himself seems at sea. He is writing to a New York specialist."

"But—but what were her injuries?"

"A slight cut on the head, one or two bruises, and—and an injury to the spine which has seemed to cause paralysis from the hips down."

A low cry came from the man. Then he asked, "And Pollyanna—how does she take it?"

"She doesn't understand at all how things really are. And I can't tell her."

"But she must know something!"

"Oh, yes. She knows she can't move. But she thinks her legs are broken. She says she's glad it's broken legs like yours rather than 'lifelong-invalids' like Mrs. Snow's, because broken legs get well, and the other—doesn't. She talks like that all the time, until it seems as if I should die!"

Through a blur of tears, the man saw Miss Polly's face twisted with emotion. "I wonder if you know, Miss Harrington, how I tried to get Pollyanna to come live with me."

"With you! Pollyanna!"

The man winced a little at the tone of her voice. But his own voice was cool when he spoke again. "Yes. I wanted to adopt her. I am very fond of Pollyanna, both for her own sake, and for her mother's. I stood ready to give Pollyanna the love that had been twenty-five years in storage."

"Love." Miss Polly remembered suddenly why she had taken this child in the first place. With a sinking heart, too, she realized something else: the dreariness of her own future now without Pollyanna. "Well?" she said.

"She would not come," he answered. "She said you had been so good to her. She wanted to stay with you—and she said she thought you wanted her to stay," he finished. He stood and turned toward the door. But instantly he heard a swift step, and found a shaking hand thrust toward him.

"When the specialist comes, and I know anything definite, I will let you hear from me," said a trembling voice. "Goodbye—and thank you for coming. Pollyanna will be pleased."

21. A WAITING GAME

On the day after John Pendleton's visit, Miss Polly prepared Pollyanna for the arrival of the specialist. "Pollyanna, my dear," she began gently, "we have decided that we want another doctor besides Dr. Warren to see you. Another one might tell us something new to do—to help you get well faster, you know."

A joyous light came to Pollyanna's face. "Dr. Chilton! Oh, Aunt Polly, I'd so love to have Dr. Chilton! I've wanted him all the time, but I was afraid you didn't, because he saw you in the sun parlor that day. So I didn't like to say anything. But I'm so glad you do want him!"

Aunt Polly's face turned white, then red, then back to white again. But when she answered, she showed very plainly that she was trying to speak lightly and cheerfully.

"Oh, no, dear! It wasn't Dr. Chilton that I meant. It is a new doctor, a very famous doctor from New York, who knows a great deal about hurts like yours."

Pollyanna's face fell. "I don't believe he knows half so much as Dr. Chilton."

"Oh, yes, he does, I'm sure, dear."

"But it was Dr. Chilton who doctored Mr. Pendleton's broken leg, Aunt Polly. If—if you don't mind very much, I would like to have Dr. Chilton—truly I would!"

Color spread over Miss Polly's face. For a moment she did not speak at all. Then she said gently, though with a touch of her old sternness, "But I do mind, Pollyanna. I mind very much. I would do anything—almost anything for you, my dear. But for reasons I do not care to speak of now, I don't wish Dr. Chilton called in on this case. And believe me, he cannot know so much about your trouble as this great doctor from New York does."

Pollyanna still looked unconvinced. "But, Aunt Polly, if you loved Dr. Chilton—"

"*What*, Pollyanna?" Aunt Polly's voice was very sharp now. Her cheeks were very red, too.

"If you loved Dr. Chilton, and didn't love the other one," sighed Pollyanna, "it seems to me that would make some difference in the good he would do. And I love Dr. Chilton."

Aunt Polly rose to her feet, a look of relief on her face.

"I am very sorry, Pollyanna," she said, a little stiffly, "but I'm afraid you'll have to let me be the judge this time. Besides, it's already arranged. The New York doctor is coming tomorrow."

As it happened, however, the New York doctor did not come. At the last moment a telegram told of a delay, because the specialist himself had fallen ill. This led Pollyanna to plead again for Dr. Chilton.

But as before, Aunt Polly shook her head and said, "No, dear." She would do anything—anything but that—to please her dear Pollyanna.

As the days of waiting passed, one by one, it did indeed seem that Aunt Polly was doing everything (but that) that she could do to please her niece.

"I wouldn't have believed it," Nancy said to Old Tom one morning. "There don't seem to be a minute in the day that Miss Polly ain't hangin' 'round waitin' to do somethin' for that blessed lamb if it ain't more than to let in the cat—and her what wouldn't let Fluff nor Buff upstairs for love nor money a week ago. Now she lets 'em tumble all over the bed just 'cause it pleases Miss Pollyanna!"

Old Tom chuckled. Then the light died from his eyes. "How is she today—the little gal?"

Nancy shook her head. "Just the same, Mr. Tom. There ain't no special difference, as I can see—or anybody, I guess. She just lays there, and tries to smile and be 'glad' 'cause the sun sets or the moon rises, or some other such thing, till it's enough to make your heart break."

"I know, it's the 'game'—bless her sweet heart!" nodded Old Tom.

"She told you, too, about that game?"

"Oh, yes. She told me long ago." The old man hesitated, and then went on. "I was growlin' one day 'cause I was so bent up and crooked. And what do you suppose the little thing said?"

"I couldn't guess. I wouldn't think she could find anythin' about that to be glad about!"

"She did. She said I could be glad, anyhow, that I didn't have to stoop so far to do my weedin' 'cause I was already bent partway over."

Those days of waiting were not easy. The doctor was nervous and impatient. Miss Polly said little, but she was growing thin and pale. Pollyanna petted the dog, smoothed the cat's sleek head, admired the flowers, ate the fruits and jellies that were sent to her, and returned cheery answers to the many messages of love that were brought to her bedside. But she, too, grew pale and thin. The poor little hands and arms moved nervously. But the once active little feet and legs now lay quiet under the blankets.

22. A Door Ajar

Everyone said that it was the cat that did it. If Fluffy had not poked a paw and nose against Pollyanna's door, the door would not have swung noiselessly open. And if the door had not been open, Pollyanna would not have heard her aunt's words.

In the hall, Dr. Warren and Miss Polly stood talking with the specialist from New York, who had arrived a week after he was first expected. Through the open door, Pollyanna clearly heard Aunt Polly's agonized exclamation.

"Not that! Doctor, not that! You don't mean the child will never walk again!"

It was all confusion then. First, from the bedroom came Pollyanna's terrified cry—"Aunt Polly, Aunt Polly!" Then Miss Polly, seeing the open door and realizing that her words had been heard, gave a low moan and, for the first time in her life, fainted.

It was Nancy who was sent to tell Mr. John Pendleton. There had been a time when Nancy would have rejoiced at the chance to see something of the House of Mystery and its master. But today her heart was too heavy to rejoice at anything.

"I'm Nancy, sir," she said respectfully when he came into the room. "Miss Harrington sent me to tell you about Miss Pollyanna."

"Well?"

"It ain't well, Mr. Pendleton," she choked.

"You don't mean—"

"Yes, sir. That doctor says—she can't walk again—never."

For a moment there was absolute silence in the room. Then the man spoke in a shaky voice. "Poor little girl! Poor little girl!"

There was another silence. Then the man asked, "She doesn't know yet—does she?"

"But she does, sir," sobbed Nancy, "and that's what makes it all the harder. She found out—drat that cat! I beg your pardon," Nancy apologized. "It's only that the cat pushed open the door and Miss Pollyanna overheard 'em talkin'."

"Poor little girl!" sighed the man again.

"Yes, sir. You'd say so, sir, if you could see her," choked Nancy. "You see it's all so fresh and new to her, and she keeps thinkin' all the time of new things she can't do. It worries her, too, 'cause she can't seem to be glad. Maybe you don't know about her game, though."

"The 'glad game'?" asked the man. "Oh, yes, she told me of that."

"Well, I guess she has told it to most folks. But you see, now she can't play it herself. She says she can't think of a thing about this not walkin' again to be glad about."

"Well, why should she?"

Nancy shifted her feet uneasily. "That's the way I felt, too, till I happened to think it would be easier if she could find somethin', you know. So I tried to—to remind her."

"To remind her! Of what?" John Pendleton's voice was impatient.

"Of—of how she told others to play it. Mis' Snow, and the rest, you know. But the poor little lamb just cries, and says it don't seem the same, somehow. She says it's easy to tell lifelong invalids how to be glad, but it ain't the same thing when you're the lifelong invalid yourself."

Nancy paused, but the man did not speak. He sat with his hand over his eyes.

"Then I tried to remind her how she used to say the game was all the nicer to play when it was hard," resumed Nancy. "But she says that it's different—when it really is hard."

It did not take long for the entire town of Beldingsville to learn that the great New York doctor had said Pollyanna Whittier would never walk again. Never before had the town been so stirred. It seemed unbelievable, impossible, cruel.

And fast on the heels of the news itself came Nancy's pitiful story that Pollyanna could not play the game—that she could not now be glad over anything.

It was then that the same thought must have, in some way, come to Pollyanna's friends. Almost at once, Miss Polly, to her great surprise, began to receive visitors: people she knew and people she did not know, men, women, and children.

Some came in and sat down for a stiff five or ten minutes. Some stood awkwardly on the porch steps, fumbling with hats or handbags. Some brought a book, a bunch of flowers, or a sweet to tempt the appetite. Some cried openly. Some turned their backs and blew their noses furiously. But all asked very anxiously about the little injured girl. And all sent to her some message.

First came Mr. John Pendleton. He came without his crutches today.

"I don't need to tell you how shocked I am," he began. "But can nothing be done?"

Miss Polly gave a gesture of despair. "Oh, Dr. Mead prescribed certain treatments and medicines. But he held out almost no hope."

John Pendleton rose abruptly—though he had but just come. His face was white, and his mouth was set into stern lines. At the door he turned. "I have a message for

Pollyanna," he said. "Tell her, please, that I have seen Jimmy Bean and that he's going to be my boy. Tell her I thought she would be—glad to know. I shall adopt him, probably."

For a brief moment Miss Polly lost her usual self-control.

"You will adopt Jimmy Bean!" she gasped.

The man lifted his chin a little. "Yes. I think Pollyanna will understand. You will tell her I thought she would be *glad!*"

"Why, of—of course," stammered Miss Polly.

"Thank you," bowed John Pendleton, as he turned to go.

In the middle of the floor Miss Polly stood, silent and amazed. She could scarcely believe what her ears had heard. John Pendleton, wealthy, independent, gloomy, known to be miserly and supremely selfish, to adopt a little boy—and a boy such as that?

With a somewhat dazed face Miss Polly went upstairs to Pollyanna's room.

"Pollyanna, I have a message for you from Mr. John Pendleton. He says to tell you he has taken Jimmy Bean for his little boy. He said he thought you'd be glad."

Pollyanna's face flamed into sudden joy. "Glad? GLAD? Oh, Aunt Polly, I've so wanted to find a place for Jimmy! I'm so glad for Mr. Pendleton, too. Now he'll have the child's presence."

"The—what?"

Pollyanna blushed. She had forgotten that she had never told her aunt of Mr. Pendleton's desire to adopt her. "The child's presence," murmured Pollyanna. "Mr. Pendleton told me once that only a woman's hand and heart or a child's presence could make a home."

"Oh, I see," said Miss Polly very gently. And she did see—more than Pollyanna realized.

Pollyanna feared that her aunt might ask further embarrassing questions, so she turned the conversation away from the Pendleton house and its master. "Dr. Chilton says so, too—that it takes a woman's hand and heart, or a child's presence, to make a home, you know," she remarked.

Miss Polly turned with a start. "Dr. Chilton! How do you know that?"

"He told me so. It was when he said he lived in just rooms, you know—not a home."

Miss Polly did not answer. Her eyes were out the window.

"So I asked him why he didn't get a woman's hand and heart, and have a home."

"Pollyanna!" Miss Polly had turned sharply. Her cheeks showed a sudden color.

"Well, I did. He looked so—so sorrowful."

"What did he say?" Miss Polly asked the question as if some force within her was urging her not to ask it.

"He didn't say anything for a minute. Then he said that you couldn't always get 'em for the asking."

There was a brief silence. Miss Polly's eyes had turned again to the window. Her cheeks were still unnaturally pink.

Pollyanna sighed. "He wants one, anyhow, I know, and I wish he could have one."

"Why, Pollyanna, how do you know?"

"Because, another day, he said something else. He said that he'd give all the world if he did have one woman's hand and heart. Why, Aunt Polly, what's the matter?"

Aunt Polly had risen hurriedly and gone to the window. "Nothing, dear," said Aunt Polly, whose whole face now was aflame.

23. THE GAME AND ITS PLAYERS

It was not long after John Pendleton's second visit that Milly Snow called one afternoon. She blushed and looked very embarrassed when Miss Polly entered the room.

"I—I came to ask about the little girl," she stammered.

"She is about the same. How is your mother?" replied Miss Polly, wearily.

"That is what I came to tell you—that is, to ask you to tell Miss Pollyanna," hurried on the girl. "We think it's so awful—so perfectly awful that the little thing can't ever walk again. And after all she's done for mother, teaching her to play the game, and all that. And when we heard how now she couldn't play it herself! I'm sure I don't see how she can, either, in her condition. But we thought if she could only know what she had done for us, that it would help, because she could be glad—that is, a little glad—" Milly stopped helplessly.

Miss Polly frowned. She would have asked what Milly meant by this "game," but there was no chance. Milly was rushing on again.

"You know nothing was ever right before—for mother. But now she lets me keep the shades up, and she takes interest in things. And she's actually begun to knit little things—baby blankets for fairs and hospitals. And she's so *glad* to think she can do it! That was all Miss Pollyanna's doings, you know, 'cause she told mother she could be glad she'd got her hands and arms, anyway. And that made mother wonder why she didn't do something

with her hands and arms. And so she began to knit. And so we want you to please tell Miss Pollyanna that it's all because of her. And please say we're so glad we know her, and we thought, maybe if she knew it, it would make her a little glad that she knew us. And—and that's all," sighed Milly, rising to her feet. "You'll tell her?"

"Why, of course," murmured Miss Polly, wondering just how much of this remarkable speech she could remember to tell.

These visits of John Pendleton and Milly Snow were only the first of many. And always there were messages about "the game" that caused Miss Polly to become more and more puzzled.

At last she confronted Nancy in the kitchen. "Nancy, will you tell me what this 'game' is that the whole town seems to be babbling about? And what, please, has my niece to do with it? Why does everybody send word to her that they're 'playing it'? As near as I can judge, half the town are stopping family quarrels, or learning to like something they never liked before, and all because of Pollyanna. Will you tell me what it all means?"

To Miss Polly's surprise, Nancy burst into tears. "It means that ever since last June that child has been makin' the whole town glad, and now they're turnin' 'round an' tryin' to make her a little glad, too."

"Glad of what?"

"Just glad! That's the game."

Miss Polly actually stamped her foot. "There you go like all the rest, Nancy. What game?"

Nancy lifted her chin. She faced her mistress and looked her squarely in the eye. "I'll tell you, ma'am. It's a game Miss Pollyanna's father learned her to play. She got a pair of crutches once in a missionary barrel when she was wantin' a doll. And she cried, of course, like any child would. Then her father told her no matter what happened, there was somethin' about it that you could be glad about, and that she could be glad about them crutches."

"Glad for crutches!" Miss Polly choked back a sob. She was thinking of the helpless little legs on the bed upstairs.

"Yes'm. That's what I said, and Miss Pollyanna said that's what she said, too. But he told her she could be glad—'cause she didn't need 'em."

"Oh!" cried Miss Polly.

"And after that she said he made a regular game of it— findin' somethin' in everythin' to be glad about. And they called it the 'just bein' glad' game. She's played it ever since."

"But, how—how—" Miss Polly came to a helpless pause.

"And you'd be surprised to find how it works, ma'am," said Nancy. "She's made me glad, too, on such a lot of things—little things, and big things. For instance, I don't mind 'Nancy' for a name half as much since she told me I could be glad it wasn't 'Hephzibah.'"

"But why hasn't she told me the game?" murmured Miss Polly. "Why has she made such a mystery of it, when I asked her?"

Nancy hesitated. "Beggin' your pardon, ma'am, you told her not to speak of her father. So she couldn't tell you. It was her father's game, you see."

Miss Polly bit her lip.

"She wanted to tell you, first off," continued Nancy. "She wanted somebody to play it with, you know. That's why I begun it, so she could have some one."

"Well, I know somebody who'll play it now," choked Miss Polly, as she turned and sped through the kitchen doorway.

Behind her, Nancy stood staring. "Well, I'll believe anythin' now," she muttered to herself. A little later, in Pollyanna's room, the nurse left Miss Polly and Pollyanna alone together.

Miss Polly forced her voice to be cheerfully matter-of-fact. "Nancy told me about the game. I think it's beautiful. I'm going to play it now—with you."

"Oh, Aunt Polly—YOU? I'm so glad! You see, I've really wanted you most of anybody, all the time."

"Yes, dear. And there are all those others, too. Why, Pollyanna, I think all the town is playing that game now with you—and the whole town is wonderfully happier—and all because of one little girl who taught the people a new game, and how to play it."

Pollyanna clapped her hands. "Oh, I'm so glad," she cried. Then, suddenly, a wonderful light shone in her face. "Why, Aunt Polly, there IS something I can be glad about, after all. I can be glad I've HAD my legs, anyway—else I couldn't have done—that!"

24. THROUGH AN OPEN WINDOW

One by one the short winter days came and went—but they were not short to Pollyanna. They were long, and sometimes full of pain. These days, however, Pollyanna was turning a cheerful face toward whatever came.

Pollyanna now, like Mrs. Snow, was knitting wonderful things out of bright colored yarns that trailed across the white spread. They made Pollyanna—again like Mrs. Snow—glad she had her hands and arms, anyway.

Pollyanna saw people now, and always there were the loving messages from those she could not see. Once she had seen John

Pendleton, and twice she had seen Jimmy Bean. John Pendleton had told her what a fine boy Jimmy was getting to be, and how well he was doing. Jimmy had told her what a first-rate home he had, and what bang-up "folks" Mr. Pendleton made. And both had said that it was all owing to her.

The winter passed, and spring came. The anxious watchers over Pollyanna's condition could see little change. There seemed every reason to believe, indeed, that Pollyanna would never walk again.

One Saturday morning, Mr. John Pendleton received a call from Dr. Thomas Chilton.

"Pendleton," began the doctor, abruptly, "I've come to you because you, better than anyone else in town, know something of my relations with Miss Polly Harrington."

John Pendleton did know something of the affair between Polly Harrington and Thomas Chilton. But the matter had not been mentioned between them for fifteen years.

"Pendleton," continued the doctor, "I want to see that child. I want to make an examination. I *must* make an examination."

"Well—can't you?"

"Can't I! Pendleton, you know very well I haven't been inside that door for more than fifteen years. The mistress of that house told me that the next time she asked me to enter it, I might take it that she was begging my pardon, and that all would be as before—which meant that she'd marry me."

"But couldn't you go without being asked?"

The doctor frowned. "Well, hardly. I have some pride, you know."

"But if you're so anxious, couldn't you swallow your pride and forget the quarrel—"

"Forget the quarrel!" interrupted the doctor. "So far as that is concerned, I'd go there on my knees—or on my head—if that would do any good. But I can't butt in and say, 'Here, take me!' can I?"

"Chilton, what was the quarrel?" demanded Pendleton.

The doctor made an impatient gesture, and got to his feet. "What was it? What's any lovers' quarrel after it's over?" he snarled, pacing the room angrily. "Pendleton, I must see that child. It may mean—I honestly believe—that Pollyanna Whittier will walk again!"

The words were spoken clearly, and they were spoken just as the doctor had almost reached the open window near John Pendleton's chair. Thus it happened that they reached the ears of a small boy kneeling beneath the window on the ground outside.

Jimmy Bean, at his Saturday morning task of pulling up the first little green weeds in the flowerbeds, sat up with ears and eyes wide open.

"Walk! Pollyanna!" John Pendleton was saying. "What do you mean?"

"I mean that from what I can hear and learn, her case is very much like one that a college friend of mine has just helped. For years he's been making this sort of thing a special study."

John Pendleton sat straight in his chair. "You must see her, man!"

The other shook his head. "But how can I, without a direct request from her aunt? Which I'll never get! She's too proud and too angry to ask me—after what she said years ago it would mean if she did ask me. But when I think of that child, and when I think that maybe in my hands lies a chance of

escape, I—" He did not finish his sentence, but with his hands thrust deep into his pockets, he turned and began to tramp up and down the room.

"But if she could be made to see—to understand," urged John Pendleton.

"Yes—but who's going to do it?" demanded the doctor.

Outside the window Jimmy Bean stirred. "Well, I know!" he whispered. *"I'm* a-goin' to do it!" He rose to his feet, crept around the corner of the house, and ran with all his might down Pendleton Hill.

25. JIMMY TAKES THE HELM

"It's Jimmy Bean. He wants to see you, ma'am," announced Nancy in the doorway.

"Me?" replied Miss Polly, plainly surprised. "Are you sure he did not mean Miss Pollyanna? He may see her a few minutes today, if he likes."

"Yes'm. I told him. But he said it was you he wanted."

"Very well, I'll come down." And Miss Polly arose from her chair a little wearily. In the sitting room she found a round-eyed, flushed-faced boy, who began to speak at once.

"Ma'am, I suppose it's dreadful, what I'm doin'. But I can't help it. It's for Pollyanna, and I'd walk over hot coals for her, or face you, or—or anythin' like that. And I think you would, too, if you thought there was a chance for her to walk again. And so that's why I come to tell you that as long as it's only pride that's keepin' Pollyanna from walkin', I knew you would ask Dr. Chilton here if you understood—"

"What?" interrupted Miss Polly, amazed.

Jimmy sighed. "There, I didn't mean to make you mad. That's why I begun by tellin' you about her walkin' again. I thought you'd listen to that."

"Jimmy, what are you talking about?"

Jimmy sighed again. "That's what I'm tryin' to tell you."

"Well, then tell me. But begin at the beginning, and be sure I understand each thing as you go. Don't plunge into the middle of it as you did before!"

"Well," said Jimmy, "to begin with, Dr. Chilton come to see Mr. Pendleton, an' they talked in the library. Do you understand that?"

"Yes, Jimmy." Miss Polly's voice was rather faint.

"Well, the window was open, and I was weedin' the flower bed under it, and I heard 'em."

"Oh, Jimmy! *Listening?*"

"It wasn't about me, and it wasn't sneak listenin'," said Jimmy. "And I'm glad I listened. You will be when I tell you. Why, it may make Pollyanna walk!"

"Jimmy, what do you mean?" Miss Polly leaned forward eagerly.

"Well, Dr. Chilton knows some doctor somewhere that can cure Pollyanna, he thinks—make her walk, you know. But he can't be sure till he sees her. And he wants to see her somethin' awful, but he told Mr. Pendleton that you wouldn't let him."

Miss Polly's face turned very red. "But, Jimmy, I—I can't— I couldn't! That is, I didn't know!" Miss Polly was twisting her fingers together helplessly.

"Yes, and that's what I come to tell you, so you would know. Now you understand?"

Miss Polly's breath came in little uneven, rapid gasps. Jimmy thought she was going to cry. But she did not cry. After a minute she said brokenly, "Yes—I'll let—Dr. Chilton—see her. Now run home, Jimmy, quick! I've got to speak to Dr. Warren. He's upstairs. I saw him drive in a few minutes ago."

A little later Dr. Warren was surprised to meet an agitated Miss Polly in the hall. He was still more surprised to hear the lady say, "Dr. Warren, you asked me once to allow Dr. Chilton to be called in, and I refused. Since then I have reconsidered. I very much desire that you should call in Dr. Chilton. Will you ask him at once—please?"

26. A NEW UNCLE

The next time Dr. Warren entered the room where Pollyanna lay, a tall, broad-shouldered man followed close behind him.

"Dr. Chilton! How glad I am to see you!" cried Pollyanna. "But, of course, if Aunt Polly doesn't want—"

"It is all right, my dear, don't worry," soothed Miss Polly, hurrying forward. "I have told Dr. Chilton that—that I want him to look you over—with Dr. Warren, this morning."

"Oh, then you asked him to come," murmured Pollyanna.

"Yes, dear, I asked him. That is—" But it was too late. The happiness that shone in Dr. Chilton's eyes was unmistakable, and Miss Polly had seen it. With very pink cheeks she turned and left the room hurriedly.

Dr. Chilton held out both his hands to Pollyanna. "Little girl, I'm thinking that one of the very gladdest jobs you ever did has been done today," he said.

At twilight a wonderfully different Aunt Polly came to Pollyanna's bedside. "Pollyanna, dear, I'm going to tell you, the very first of all. Someday I'm going to give Dr. Chilton to you for your uncle. And it's you that have done it all. Oh, Pollyanna, I'm so happy! And so—glad!"

Pollyanna began to clap her hands. But even as she brought her small palms together the first time, she stopped, and held them suspended.

"Aunt Polly, Aunt Polly, were *you* the woman's hand and heart he wanted so long ago? You were—I know you were! And that's what he meant by saying I'd done the gladdest job of all today. I'm so glad! Why, Aunt Polly, I'm so glad that I don't mind—even my legs, now!"

Aunt Polly swallowed a sob. "Perhaps, some day, dear—" She did not finish. Aunt Polly did not dare to tell, yet, the great hope that Dr. Chilton had put into her heart. But she did say this: "Pollyanna, next week you're going to take a journey. On a nice comfortable little bed you're going to be carried in cars and carriages to a great doctor who has a big house many miles from here. He's a friend of Dr. Chilton's, and we're going to see what he can do for you."

27. WHICH IS A LETTER FROM POLLYANNA

Dear Aunt Polly and Uncle Tom:

Oh, I can—I can—I CAN walk! I did today all the way from my bed to the window! It was six steps. My, how good it was to be on legs again!

All the doctors stood around and smiled, and all the nurses stood beside them and cried. A lady in the next ward who walked last week peeked into the door, and another one who hopes she can walk next month was invited in, and she clapped her hands.

I don't see why the nurses cried. I wanted to sing and shout and yell! Oh—oh—oh! just think, I can walk—walk—WALK! Now I don't mind being here almost ten months, and I didn't miss the wedding, anyhow. Wasn't that just like you, Aunt Polly, to come here and get married right beside my bed, so I could see you. You always do think of the gladdest things!

Pretty soon, they say, I shall go home. I wish I could walk all the way there. I don't think I shall ever want to ride anywhere anymore. It will be so good just to walk. Oh, I'm so glad! I'm glad for everything. Why, I'm glad now I lost my legs for a while, for you never, never know how perfectly lovely legs are till you haven't got them—ones that go, I mean. I'm going to walk eight steps tomorrow.

> *With heaps of love to everybody,*
> *Pollyanna*